"I don't know what it's going to take to prove your innocence, but we're going to do it! You've got to trust me now."

"I...I don't have any choice, Jericho. You're all I've got."

The enormity of her words filled him with a warm, heated glow that seemed to emanate from low in his stomach, spreading out to singe his limbs and scorch his heart. His entire life, until this moment, had been a solitary, empty existence.

Until Vera reached deep into his soul and touched him with a sweet, golden intimacy so freely given. "Don't do that," he growled. "Don't put that kind of responsibility on my shoulders."

"The only thing I'm asking of you," she whispered, "is that you don't abandon me. Don't leave me to face this alone."

Fear and uncertainty melted into physical, primal need. Churning, demanding want for this woman filled his belly. He pulled her into his arms. His mouth lowered to capture hers, soft, yielding and filled with an urgency as raw and compelling as his own....

Dear Reader,

Some of you might not know that I divide my time between our home in the suburbs of San Diego and an isolated forty-acre "ranch" in the Arizona mountains. Recently, while in the small town near our ranch, I noticed a sexy cowboy leaning against the wall—a gun strapped to his hip. (Yes, it's still legal to carry a sidearm in Arizona.) That Old West independence was so evident in his stance that I realized how difficult it would be for him to fit into a Southern California lifestyle.

Maybe even more disconcerting, I thought, would be to take one of those citified Californians and move *her* to the Old West. That was the germ for *Jackson's Woman*.

I hope you enjoy Vera McBride's adventure as she travels through time and ends up, wanted for murder, in 1896 Jerome, Arizona. Only with the dubious help of the very distracting gambler, Jericho Jackson, does she have a chance of clearing her name and finding a way back to the future. But will she be able to leave Jericho behind?

I love hearing from my readers. Please drop me a line at P.O. Box 2571, La Mesa, CA 91943.

Happy reading!

Jodi Lind

Jackson's Woman
Judi Lind

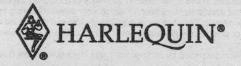

HARLEQUIN®

TORONTO • NEW YORK • LONDON
AMSTERDAM • PARIS • SYDNEY • HAMBURG
STOCKHOLM • ATHENS • TOKYO • MILAN • MADRID
PRAGUE • WARSAW • BUDAPEST • AUCKLAND

This one's for my good buddy Sharon Ihle,
who's held my hand every step of the way.
Your counsel, friendship and irreverent humor
are treasured.

ISBN 0-373-22504-0

JACKSON'S WOMAN

Copyright © 1999 by Judith A. Lind

Printed in U.S.A.

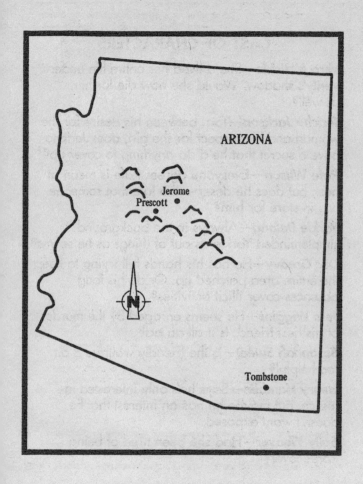

CAST OF CHARACTERS

Vera McBride—She'd lived her entire life under Verity's shadow. Would she now die for her, as well?

Jericho Jackson—Torn between his desire for the woman and his respect for the girl, does Jericho have a secret that he'd do *anything* to cover up?

Rafe Wilson—Everyone agrees Rafe is mean at best, but does he deserve the fate that someone has in store for him?

Yorkie Delong—Always in the background, is simpleminded Yorkie as out of things as he seems?

Doc Greavy—He has his hands full trying to keep the entire area patched up. Or do his long absences cover illicit activities?

Jess Wiggins—He seems enraged by the murder of his best friend. Is it all an act?

Susannah Sweet—Is the friendly waitress a bit *too* helpful?

Henry Hamblin—Says he's only interested in justice, but maybe he has an interest that he doesn't want exposed.

Sally Weaver—Had she been tired of being Rafe's lover?

Prologue

Jerome, Arizona, 1896

Verity McBride leaned against the unpainted shack to shift her burden and catch her breath. Her arms were scratched and aching with the weight of the firewood she was toting. With her mother being so frail since the baby's birth, most of the household chores had fallen onto the young woman's shoulders. Although, she acknowledged with a grateful sigh, soon Tad and Josiah would be old enough to help out.

Icy fingers of night wind crept through her cotton dress and she pushed herself away from the wall. She'd better stop daydreaming and get back inside before she froze solid, she thought ruefully as she trudged around the corner of the house.

Verity stopped, held in place by the sight in front of her. Rafe's horse, Duke, still saddled and bridled, was tied to the front stoop. That told her one thing: Rafe Wilson was home and drunk. Almost the kindest thing a body could say about her stepfather was that he was ornery on occasion. When he was liquored up, though, he was meaner than a cornered badger and bullied anyone in his path. With one notable exception: Rafe loved his horse.

All the compassion and kindness he failed to show his fellow humans was showered on Duke. The only time Rafe neglected to take care of that horse was when he was mean drunk and itching for a fight.

Now the animal stood in front of her, still saddled and panting from a hard ride. Immutable proof that Rafe had drank his fill of cheap whiskey and was waiting inside.

Nausea clutched Verity's stomach and she quietly laid down her bundle of wood. No longer feeling the bitter cold wind, she slowly inched toward the cabin. Lately, it had become harder and harder to keep out of her stepfather's grasp. Her greatest fear was that one day she wasn't going to be able to elude his filthy advances.

But she couldn't leave her mother and the boys alone with him.

She glanced over her shoulder. What she wouldn't give to turn and run back to the shelter of the barn and hide in a pile of clean, warm hay. Another blast of cold skittered under her skirt tail and a frigid chill whispered up her bare legs.

Forcing one foot before the other, she edged toward the front door.

As she stepped onto the stoop, she could hear Rafe's voice filling the night air. Screaming and cursing. She knew before she looked through the window that his fist would be flailing the air as he advanced toward the cowering form of her mother.

Verity gulped deeply as a cold dread seeped into

her bones. Her mother's people believed in signs and omens; the howling wind and her sick stomach were omen enough of trouble, bad trouble, waiting for Verity inside the ramshackle shanty.

Her trembling fingers lifted the latch and she entered the cabin. From the corner of her eye, she could see the little ones huddled under the window—waiting out the storm. Her mother's face already bore the crimson imprint of Rafe's hand across her smooth cheek.

Suddenly, Verity was filled with a seething, boiling white rage. Scarcely aware she was moving, she crossed the room and yanked the cast iron skillet off the stove. Like a sleepwalker, she silently stepped between her mother and Rafe.

As if noticing her for the first time, he wobbled on his feet and snarled, "What's your problem, Missy?"

"You're drunk. Leave my mother alone and go sleep it off."

"Oh, aren't we gettin' to be the high-and-mighty one?" Now ignoring his hapless spouse, he focused his foul temper on Verity. "I said I want some beef-steak. Since it's too much for a man to expect his wife to fix him some supper, I guess you'll have to do it, Missy."

Verity's arm burned with the strain of holding the heavy skillet above her head, but she couldn't back down. "There's no meat, Rafe. Maybe if you fed your family as good as you do that horse—"

"Seems to me that I fed your skinny rear all these years! Now I said to get me some meat on the table."

He shook his clenched fist, his huge knuckles stopping only inches from her face.

Through a red haze of fear and fury, Verity heard her mother begging her not to antagonize him, but the time for backing down had passed. Squaring her shoulders, she said coldly, "We had beans and biscuits for supper. Again. If you want some, I'll heat them up. There's nothing else, so if you don't want that—"

Bellowing like a wounded bear, Rafe's whiskey-soaked breath clogged her nostrils. "I guess you'll be wantin' to feel my strap again."

Verity involuntarily stepped back, but held her chin high as she tried to quell the terror that was threatening to choke her. "You'll not be hitting me or anyone else in this house, Rafe Wilson. Not tonight, not ever. Your bullying days are finished."

To show him the seriousness of her resolve, she swung the skillet in an arc, barely missing his grizzled chin. Hesitantly, he lurched forward, his expression suddenly sly but wary.

"I mean it, Rafe. Stay back!" Verity's shoulder muscles screamed with the weight of the cocked skillet.

"Oh, so we're all growed up, now, is that right? Growed up enough to threaten a man in his own home, so you must be woman enough to give a man a little lovin'." He wobbled forward, arms outstretched.

"Rafe, I'm warning you. Stop now."

As if she'd issued a challenge, he reared his head

back and laughed aloud. "Now why won't you give your ole' pa a little sugar? C'mere, girl."

When she sensed he was about to lunge, Verity swung again, hoping to startle him into backing off. But Rafe stepped directly into the path of the skillet and it struck his head with a sickening thwack.

She stood in helpless dismay as blood gushed from the gaping wound on his temple. Overcome with horror, she watched silently as his eyes rolled back in his head and he collapsed in a crumpled heap onto the dirt floor.

The pan dropped from her numb fingers.

Handing the baby to Tad, her mother, Min-e-wah, ran and knelt beside the fallen man. Her slim brown fingertips probed his eyelids, the side of his throat. Her black eyes wide with alarm, Min-e-wah lowered her head onto Rafe's too still chest.

Finally, she looked up, all the pain of her life mirrored in her stricken eyes. She spoke at last, her voice only a whisper but loud as a scream in the still cabin. "Oh, Verity, he's not breathing. You've killed him."

No! It couldn't be, Verity thought. She'd never meant to kill him. Only frighten him into leaving them alone!

For a long moment the two women stared at each other without speaking. They both understood that it didn't matter that Rafe Wilson had been a no-account brawler, and that more people would rather see him dead than alive. Verity was only a woman; and, even worse, half Apache. In this savage land she counted for less than a horse or a faithful dog. She'd be charged with murder. At best, she'd spend years in a

squalid prison. At worst…well, that didn't bear thinking about.

There was only one thing to do. Run. Get away.
Hide out until the law forgot all about Rafe Wilson
and his half-breed stepdaughter.

Dashing to the cupboard, she pulled out a pair of
work denims, one of Rafe's old shirts and a heavy
jacket. Silently, her mother filled a sack with biscuits
and a tin of dried beef she'd kept hidden to provide
protein for her children during the long, barren winter.

"Where will you go?" Min-e-wah asked, covering
Rafe's still form with a stained and torn sheet.

There was only one place Verity could think of to
hide out, and only one person who might help her.
"The line shack at the Balbriggan." She knew Rafe
usually kept the rickety shack stocked with supplies
since he used it for elk hunting. And for drunken par-
ties with his whores from Rosie's Sporting House.

Everyone would expect a fugitive half-Indian girl
to run back to her mother's tribe; no one would look
for her at the old Balbriggan Mine. Seven miles from
Jerome, its copper had played out nearly three years
ago and it lay discarded like a broken toy.

"You have to get word to Mr. Jackson. Tell
him…no, don't tell him anything. Just ask him to
come talk to me."

Min-e-wah shook her head doubtfully and took the
squalling infant from Tad's arms. "He's a good man,
daughter, but…"

Verity understood what her mother didn't want to
say. No white man, not even Jericho Jackson, could
be counted on to help a half-breed, especially against

a murder charge. But he was her only hope. "I...I don't know what else to do, Mother. Just get word to him, let him know where I am. I have to trust someone. Then you must take the boys and go back to our people. You and the children will be safe there."

Min-e-wah nodded, her dark eyes damp with unshed tears. "Go quickly, daughter. May the spirits guide your path and keep you safe."

Wiping a sudden tear from her own eye, Verity dragged a worn quilt from one of the bunks and slung it over her shoulder. Holding her most prized possession, her journal, against her breast, she mouthed a goodbye to Min-e-wah and strode out the door.

Pausing on the porch, she took a last glance at the hovel that had been her home for so many years.

Using the horse as a buffer between her and the blustering wind shrilling down the mountain, she stuffed her scant belongings into her stepfather's saddlebags. Refusing to hear the panic welling up inside her, Verity pulled the denim trousers beneath her skirt and shrugged into Rafe's jacket.

She cast a bittersweet glance at the cabin and hauled herself onto Duke's back. Clicking her tongue softly, she eased the animal onto the narrow trail, praying silently that she would make it to Balbriggan Mine before the approaching storm claimed her.

Chapter One

Jerome, Arizona, the present

"And here, ladies and gentlemen, is the pride of old Jerome, the legendary Balbriggan Mine." The tour guide, resplendent in cowboy attire, right down to his battered Stetson and drooping mustache, climbed out of the minivan.

The seven tourists accompanying him also alighted and stretched their weary muscles in the blinding Arizona sunlight.

Vera McBride jumped down and wiped her grimy palms on the seat of her jeans. After absorbing the warmth of the sun's rays for a moment, she tossed her denim jacket back in the van. Although the last two nights had been cold, the days were still warm. A far cry from the blustery, gray winter weather of northern California. Although at this high altitude, she knew severe snowstorms were as common as the blazing heat she always associated with Arizona.

Popping on her sunglasses, she stared around in surprise. She had expected to feel a stirring, some kinship with the past but...but the Balbriggan only evoked a sense of melancholy. A sadness for answers that might never be found.

Stuffing the journal that had started her on this quest into her backpack, Vera took a few halting steps toward the other six passengers who had gathered around their guide.

Vera frowned as Jeffrey, a quarrelsome boy of perhaps ten and the youngest member of the group, pulled away from his mother. Thrusting his chin forward in yet another overt challenge, Jeffrey sneered. "How come this place is so famous? Looks like a dump to me."

The tour guide raised an eyebrow but forced a smile at the youngster. "The Balbriggan's special, boy. During its heyday in 1889, roughly four tons of copper ore were hauled out of here every week. Unfortunately, the vein was shallow and the Balbriggan only rang up a profit for about seven years, but somehow this old dig captures the spirit of the Old West."

"Why is that?" Jeffrey's mother placed a restraining hand on her son's shoulder.

Leading his charges toward the newly reinforced entrance, the guide said, "Folks claim to see spirits around here."

He suddenly had Jeffrey's attention. And Vera's as well. "Spirits?" she echoed.

"He means ghosts, don'tcha?" Jeffrey interrupted.

"That's right, son."

"What kind of ghosts? Bank robbers and Indians?"

The guide chuckled. "Not exactly. No, folks claim

that the ghost of Verity McBride walks these hills when the moon's high.''

Vera started. She shouldn't be surprised that Verity was something of a local legend, based on what she'd read in her distant relation's journal. But it was still a mild shock to hear a complete stranger speaking so matter-of-factly about the ancestor Vera had come to think of as her own private link with the past.

Jeffrey's lip curled again as he wiped grimy hands on his white T-shirt. ''A girl? You mean the famous ghost is a dumb old girl?''

''Nothing wrong with girls, son. You just wait a couple years. But I don't guess you're very interested in hearing about a ghost. Let's talk about mine statistics instead—''

''No!'' Jeffrey interjected, inadvertently vocalizing the feelings of the rest of the group.

Their guide, while thorough and knowledgeable, was prone to quoting numbers and dates. Vera knew they'd all rather hear the legend of Verity McBride than another meaningless statistic.

The guide cocked his stained Stetson on the back of his head. ''You sure? I don't want to bore you.'' His eyes twinkled as he teased the boy.

Jeffrey planted his feet and crossed his arms. ''Yeah, tell me about that ghost woman.''

Propping his foot on a rock, the guide lowered his voice. ''Verity McBride was a half-breed accused of murdering her stepfather. Those who knew her claimed it was impossible. Verity had the face of an angel and the prettiest long black hair ever seen. Like this lady's hair.''

He smiled and pointed to Vera's own ink-dark hair, tied in a loose ponytail at her nape. Then, his smile melted. "Say, are you all right, miss? You look a little pale."

"What? Oh, no, I'm fine. Not used to the heat, I guess." As if to validate her words, Vera wiped a sheen of perspiration from her brow. It felt so odd, hearing this stranger speak about Verity as if he'd known her. That was ridiculous, of course. Verity's last journal entry had been made over a hundred years ago. Just before she disappeared. Her legend had grown like wildfire until Verity's story was as well-known as that of Paul Bunyan—at least, in this tiny mountainside village.

A story Vera knew as well as her own. The legend of Verity McBride had followed Vera like a dark, stalking vapor for most of her life. In fact, the night Vera was born, her mother had dreamed of Verity, a dream in which Verity vowed to protect the infant from danger throughout her life.

That dream, along with Vera's uncanny likeness to the only surviving photo of her distant relative, and the similarities in their names had caused family members to lower their voices to a whisper whenever Vera entered the room. An only child in a world of adults, she'd even believed their teasing that she wasn't "real," but a reincarnation of their long-dead relation.

Now, she was finally in Jerome, Arizona, at the abandoned mine where Verity had last been seen alive. Maybe now Vera would find the answers that hadn't been in the journal she'd treasured for so long.

Maybe even free herself from the haunting spirit that had dominated her life.

The guide glanced at his wristwatch. "Time's getting away from us, folks. I'll finish Verity's story on the way back to town. Right now, let's go inside. Everybody got your flashlights handy?" He paused while they all held up the pencil-point lights he'd handed out earlier.

"Good. There's no electric power in the mine, so keep those lights pointed at the path in front of you so you don't trip on any debris. Keep your eye on my light so no one gets lost. Got it?"

They all mumbled their assent and he switched on a powerful portable beam as he herded his group into the dim mine. "I want everyone to stick close to me. Including you, Jeffrey. There's a lot of twists and turns in this old shaft and some of them haven't been reinforced yet."

Their voices hushed as they entered the cool, dim interior. Only the guide's occasional terse directive could be heard over the soft slap of shoe leather as they trailed along the packed dirt floor.

Lagging a few feet behind the others, Vera was lost in her own thoughts, occasionally focusing her penlight on the dank red earth walls. According to the journal, Verity had hidden in this very mine to escape "justice" from the law after Rafe Wilson's death. She'd only been nineteen. Had she shrunk back in terror when daylight faded and she was alone in the darkness?

How many days had she hidden in these treacherous depths?

And what had ultimately become of her?

When the posse finally tracked her down after Verity's stepfather's body was discovered, they found the Balbriggan deserted. The only evidence Verity had been there at all was the rumpled quilt and dog-eared journal she'd left behind. Had Verity escaped to live out her life in peace and obscurity, or had she gotten lost in the twisted maze of Balbriggan's many tunnels and met her death through cold and starvation?

The answer, like the lovely half-Indian maiden, had disappeared into time.

The soft drone of the guide's voice echoed down the empty shaft. Vera looked up. The others had disappeared around a bend. She'd better catch up before she, too, was lost.

Hitching the knapsack strap onto her shoulder, she hurried to rejoin the others. A quick darting shadow down a side tunnel caught her attention. She stopped and stared into the murky darkness. A sliver of white moved then disappeared again.

"Jeffrey? Is that you?" Vera called into the dingy corridor. Her voice trailed away in the hollow emptiness.

She inched forward. They were so far from the entrance that it was almost pitch-dark. Eerily, hauntingly dark. "Jeffrey?" Was that quaking voice really hers?

Suddenly, another flash of white raced away, but not before she'd raised her penlight and captured the youngster's face above his white T-shirt. "This isn't funny, Jeffrey. Come on back before you get lost. Where's your mother?"

The boy didn't respond.

Vera glanced behind her. No beckoning light from the guide's flashlight, nor murmur of voices penetrated the emptiness. If she went for help, Jeffrey could be well and truly lost, or injured, before she returned. Besides, her years of experience as a California Highway Patrol officer had conditioned her to respond quickly to potential emergencies. The most expeditious course of action was to go after the mischievous adolescent and drag him back to his doting mother.

If she didn't throttle him first.

Fists on hips, Vera advanced deeper into the blackness. "Jeffrey, do you hear me? The joke's over...time to go back to the others."

In the distance she heard the creak of ancient lumber.

"Jeffrey! Come on back before you get hurt. Don't make me come after you." If the boy's mother didn't get control of the willful child soon, Vera reflected, the boy was headed for trouble when puberty kicked in. She shuddered in memory of the multitude of teenage "Jeffreys" she'd pulled from automobile wreckage.

Whether or not it was politically correct to reprimand someone else's youngster, Vera intended to give young Jeffrey a severe tongue-lashing when she finally caught up with him.

Step after halting step, Vera continued to chide the youngster while she followed the minute sounds of his passage. Her scolding, she knew, was more like whistling in the dark than actual anger. This old mine might be the source of a notorious family legend, but it was still spooky. Wooden planks that occasionally littered the dirt floor wobbled precariously beneath her feet as, keeping her fingertips on the earthen walls, she followed the small, scuffling sounds of Jeffrey's footfall.

She rounded another curve and a dank, acrid smell rose like fumes from a cyanide pellet dropped in acid.

Playing her penlight across the flooring, she saw a chalky white substance coating the floor and walls. A by-product from the copper?

Vera jumped at a slight scuffling over head. Shining her light upward, she shuddered at the dark, softly undulating mass squirming along the rafters. Bats! The nocturnal creatures began softly squealing at the intrusion and the noxious odor became even more pronounced. Vera jerked her hand from the bat guano covering the wall, swiped it across her jeans and held her forearm over her mouth and nose. The fetid odor was almost overwhelming.

Anxious to get out of the bats' territory, she pressed onward. Finally, the smell faded and she knew she was beyond the bats' lair. But where were the others? Why hadn't they noticed the missing pair and come looking? And where was Jeffrey? It had been several minutes since she'd last spotted any movement in the mine.

When she saw his mother again, she intended to give her some strong advice on the care and taming of ten-year-old boys. Irritated to reckless anger, Vera stalked forward and came down on a rotted board.

Squealing in protest at the sudden weight, the plank buckled and Vera felt herself start to sway. She glanced down and gasped in dismay. She'd somehow ventured onto a wooden catwalk of sorts. At least half of the boards were missing, while several others were broken into jagged scraps. The only safeguard was a badly frayed rope that had been looped around a few sagging posts as a makeshift railing.

Tightly grasping the penlight in her shaky fingers, she pointed the beam downward but its feeble light couldn't penetrate the depth of the shaft. At least the utter darkness below kept her from seeing exactly how far down she would fall if the catwalk gave way.

Creak! The rickety bridge bucked ferociously. Vera's hand flailed the air as she grasped for support. But she'd moved too far from the wall and her fingers no longer found purchase.

As she rocked on the wobbly, moaning timbers she thought suddenly of Verity McBride, and had an image of the young woman standing beside her, wrapping a protective arm around her shoulders. Stunned by the vividness of the hallucination, Vera redoubled her efforts to find a handhold.

Lunging against the red dirt wall, she drew in a quick breath when she struck something hard and metallic. She grabbed, clutching at a bright silvery horseshoe nailed to a soot-blackened beam. Even in her panic, she was taken aback by the horseshoe's similarity to one that had always hung over her mother's mantle. For good luck.

She could certainly use some of that luck right now, she thought, as she clutched the sweat-slickened metal. Her forearms strained until she thought her arm would surely pull from the socket but she didn't give in to the fatigue.

Suddenly, the horseshoe dipped downward, jerking free from Vera's grasp. A white swirling mist seemed to envelop her, and a cavalcade of dizzying stars exploded behind her eyes.

Even Verity's protective spirit couldn't defeat the rotted lumber. With a crack, the remaining floorboards broke away and Vera fell backward, spiraling into the black nothingness far below, where she landed with a bone-jarring thud.

VERA DIDN'T KNOW how long she'd lain, drifting in and out of consciousness, in the musty pit. She had a vague sense of someone beside her, someone dressed in white, holding her head and whispering soothing words. Jeffrey? No, certainly not the spoiled, willful child who'd gotten her into this mess.

Probably a hallucination brought on by the fall.

She turned slightly and realized her head was resting on her backpack and that a blanket or soft cloth was draped across her body. Had she become entangled in an old piece of fabric when she fell? Or…had someone covered her against the cold?

If so, why had she been left alone in this pit? Verity's journal was wedged in a pocket, where it had been before.

Struggling onto her elbows, Vera cringed against the tenderness of muscles strained by the fall. Drawing on her emergency medical training, she cautiously tested her fingers, then arms and finally her legs. Her hands and elbows were scraped raw, and her face felt caked with centuries-old dirt. But other than being bruised and sore, everything seemed to be in working order. She decided to risk sitting up.

A major mistake. Her head pounded like a thousand hammers were beating out an endless supply of horseshoes on invisible anvils. Slowly raising her hand, Vera gingerly examined her scalp, amazed by the number and variety of bumps and knots her probing fingers encountered. The cushion of her backpack probably kept her from being killed.

Or was a slow, lingering death her destiny? The grim thought reminded her that the mine had been abandoned for decades and was used only by the occasional tour company. Even so, she'd wandered far from the normal route. The earthen walls would absorb the sound of her voice, so that if her rescuers were more than a few feet away they'd never hear her call.

Vera shuddered beneath the realization that the pit she was lying in might well become her coffin.

No! She couldn't just give up. She had a life. Her cat Squiggles would never adjust to living with Sheila and her shar-pei. And what about Vera's mother? Even though the older woman, bedridden now with Alzheimer's disease, hadn't recognized her daughter in months, wouldn't she miss her only child's visits?

Besides, Vera wasn't a quitter.

She'd had to work harder and longer than the men in her class at the academy just to pass the grueling physical. But hadn't she ultimately been accepted as a patrol officer for the CHP? Vera hadn't overcome so many obstacles to just give up and die now.

She licked her lips, suddenly aware of her dry mouth. She wouldn't last long without water, and the temperature in the deserted mine would surely drop dramatically as night approached. That cotton quilt might not be enough to stave off the cold. Hot tears stung her eyelids and she bit down on her lip to keep from crying. She couldn't give in to fear, and she *wouldn't* just lie still and die of thirst or hypothermia.

Nor could she rely on the possibility of help; she had to find her own way out.

The flashlight! She had to find it. Refusing to give in to the fear that was threatening to engulf her, Vera trailed her fingertips over the floor. Her palms were raw and oozing and the tiny pebbles littering the floor stung like needles poking her bruised flesh. But she had to have that flashlight. Had to.

At last, as her eyes adjusted to the darkness, she glimpsed the slender cylinder a few inches from her hand. Her fingers clutched the cold metal and she clutched the penlight to her chest. Flicking the switch with her thumb, her heart sank when no reassuring glow followed.

Vera batted the head of the light against her palm and flicked the switch time and again. It was useless; the penlight had been broken in the fall. She was alone in the darkness.

A cold, sodden fear filled her soul. Never had she felt more alone, more helpless, in her life. The life that had seemed so empty, so meaningless a few weeks ago but now seemed more precious than gold.

There had to be a way out of this pit. And she would find it.

After a few moments, the hammers echoing in her head eased a bit. Encouraged, she decided to try standing. Like a moth shedding its cocoon, she unwrapped herself from the cotton covering and eased onto her feet. Although weak and wobbly, her legs held and she forced herself to remain standing. A wave of dizziness wrapped her in its folds and she swayed, reaching out for something to steady her. Her hand found nothing in the pitch darkness, but suddenly, Vera had a sense of unseen hands clutching her shoulders, protecting her from further harm.

She drew deep breaths through her open mouth, while the unseen hands held her until the wave of dizziness finally eased. Her arms clutched around her own waist, Vera leaned against those strong hands, real or imagined, that were her only comfort. Her only security.

The nausea finally dissipated, leaving Vera weak but grateful anew that she'd survived the fall. Slowly turning to see what she was leaning against, she had an odd sense of movement behind her, and suddenly, the support was gone and she once more felt alone in the black emptiness.

Glancing upward at the faint ambient light filtering around the broken catwalk, she wondered why no one was calling her name. Why weren't they looking for her? Of course, she had no idea how long she'd been unconscious. They could have been searching for hours. They might have given up.

No!

She mustn't give in to her fears. The others wouldn't abandon her. Vera remembered the cottony fabric and reached down to pull it up to her chest. Someone *had* covered her. Her rescuer had probably gone for help.

"Hello? Anyone up there?"

Only an empty, haunting stillness responded. The

erratic thudding of her own heartbeat resounded like a frenetic drum in the hollow silence.

Refusing to believe she was alone, Vera reflected that her voice had sounded weak, rusty, even to her own ears. She'd have to shout louder for the sound to carry throughout the vast cavernous structure. Brushing a strand of hair from her mouth, she cleared her throat and tried again.

"Hello! Can you hear me? I've fallen and can't get out." An incongruous giggle of mounting hysteria tickled her throat. She sounded like that old lady on the television commercial; the one who'd fallen and couldn't get up. Why had she ever found that commercial remotely amusing? There was certainly nothing funny about a person lying helpless on the ground.

Nonetheless, a fresh chuckle burbled up from her chest and broke loose as she joined in the laugh fate was surely enjoying at her expense. This trip to Arizona was for the sole purpose of discovering what had become of Verity McBride. Vera's research had brought her to the Balbriggan where Verity had disappeared decades ago; would Vera also meet her destiny in this abandoned mine?

Alone, frightened and hungry. Like Verity.

But Vera wasn't giving up; not without a fight.

Her will to live strengthened by encroaching panic, she cupped her hands around her mouth and drew in a deep breath. Using every fiber of her reserve of strength, she filled her lungs and shouted, "Hello! Can you hear me?"

"I've heard freight trains that made less racket."

Vera jumped at the sound of a rich, masculine voice. Because of the odd configuration of the criss-crossing tunnels, she couldn't tell from which direction the man had spoken. But energized by the fact that she wasn't alone, that help was on the way, she grinned and shouted again, "Did anyone ever tell you that you have the most beautiful voice on earth?"

A pause, then a droll chuckle sounded in the vast emptiness. "Not so's I recall. But keep talking so I can track you."

To converse with that deep, welcome voice required no effort at all. "You don't know how glad I was to hear you. I thought they'd all gone off and left me here."

"All who?" He was closer now. "Who'd you think had abandoned you? Ver, you don't have the boys here, do you?"

Boys? Maybe he meant Jeffrey, the youngster she'd been chasing when she fell. "No, I was talking about the people from the tour. The ones I came with."

There was a long silence. When her rescuer spoke again, his voice boomed with nearness. "By any chance did you hit your head when you fell?"

Vera recalled that relief map of goose eggs on her scalp. "Maybe a mild bump or two."

Suddenly, a flickering light appeared overhead and the silhouette of a man's head bobbed over the edge of the pit. "That explains it then," he muttered, his voice not quite so melodious as before. "You've gone and knocked yourself silly."

Chapter Two

Jericho Jackson tipped his hat to the back of his head and lifted the lantern over the mine shaft. She was standing on a rock ledge about nine feet below the bridge. If she'd fallen a yard farther in any direction, she would have plunged another hundred feet to her sure death.

Certain that the girl had no idea how close she was standing to eternity, he decided to keep his tone light-hearted and nonthreatening. At least until he hauled her to safety. Then he might just wring her pretty little neck.

"Good to know your mouth still works, but what about the rest of you? Any damage?"

"N-no. Nothing major. A few bumps and scrapes. Where's everyone else?"

Momentarily confused, he finally realized she must be concerned that he'd been followed. And with damn good cause. "I came alone. Just like your message said."

"My message?"

"Yeah, the boy reached me a couple hours ago. I came right away."

"Are you with the search-and-rescue unit?"

He pondered that question for a long moment, and finally decided her head injury must be more severe than he'd first thought. She *sounded* lucid, but then she'd go and say something that made absolutely no sense. Deciding the wisest course was to humor her until he could get her to safety, Jericho bobbed his head. "Yeah. Search and rescue, that's me."

"Thank God."

She wouldn't be so thankful when she realized he was only saving her to swing from the hangman's noose. Right now, though, he'd best concentrate on getting her out of that pit.

Looking around, Jericho spied a sturdy-looking spike embedded in one of the remaining beams. He looped the lantern handle over it, and hunkered down over the pit again. "Listen, Ver, I'm going to have to go back outside for some rope."

"Why didn't you bring it in with you?"

Jericho bit his lip. "If I'd known you were going to hide out at the bottom of a mine shaft, I would've. But, listen, I want you to take two more steps toward me, then sit back down."

"Why can't you hoist me up from here?"

"Dammit, woman, will you stop arguing and just do what I say."

He could only see the glitter of her dark eyes and the outline of her fists jammed against her hips, but she finally conceded and followed his instructions. "Now what?" she asked, with a hint of sarcasm.

"Now you just sit there 'til I get back. You're rest-ing on a rock ledge jutting out of the wall. If you'd stepped backward another couple feet, you probably wouldn't have touched bottom this side of China.''

He heard her quick intake of breath, and saw her head whip around toward the murky emptiness behind her. Satisfied that she would stay put until he returned, Jericho grabbed the lantern and quickly retraced his steps to the mine entrance.

In minutes he was back, a length of rope tucked under his right arm. He set the lantern back on the post and scanned the area for a nearby beam sturdy enough to bear her weight. Finding a likely-looking timber, he tied one end of the hemp to the post. If his hand slipped, at least she wouldn't fall too far.

After a couple of tugs to make sure the knots would hold, he fashioned a loose slipknot on the other end and swung it over the edge of the pit. "Now, step into that loop and draw it up around your waist. It'll ride up under your arms and that's fine, just make sure it's secure. Got it?''

A faint rustling and a couple of grunts later, she tugged on the rope. "Ready.''

Jericho knew it would take tremendous hand strength to haul even her slight body up that steep wall. While he figured he was strong enough, he decided to try an old horse wrangler's trick as added insurance. Years ago he'd watched a slightly built cowpoke hold a wild-eyed stallion by pressing his lariat against his thighs. The extra friction of the rope on his denims was just enough to stop the horse.

Ought to be enough to raise a nervous filly. "Okay, I'm going to give three hard yanks and then stop for a breath. When I pull you, brace your feet against the wall and start walking up to meet me."

"Don't you have a winch? Or a pulley?"

Lord, what was wrong with her? She sends a frantic message for him to meet her at an abandoned mine, then expects him to show up with pulleys, ropes and a home-cooked meal. "No, sugar, all I've got is a willing mood and that's fading fast. Now, you ready to come up?"

"Yes," she answered meekly, and he wrapped the hemp's slack around his waist and started to pull her up, one sweat-popping inch at a time.

Although she was heavier than he expected, the first three pulls were accomplished without a hitch. But in the middle of the next attempt, Jericho stepped backward into a small damp spot and slid onto his rump.

"Ow!" A shrill cry from the girl verified she'd slipped back down to the starting point.

Regaining his feet, he tightened up the slack on the rope. "You all right down there?"

"F-fine, except for the rope burns on my...upper body. What happened?"

"A little slip and I landed on my caboose."

"Are you sure you shouldn't go get some more help? Maybe the fire department has a portable ladder."

Fire department? Jerome *did* have a fire brigade of sorts. The ramshackle wooden structures, and the close proximity of the town buildings to one another, made fire an ever present danger. But what they had was a wagon that carried a one-hundred-gallon barrel drum of water and a brass bell. At the first sign of smoke, somebody yanked on the bell and every able-bodied soul in town came running. If the bell rang long enough, even the brothels and Jericho's saloon emptied out.

But of what possible use did she think the volunteer fire brigade could be? A good many of them had been drinking buddies with Rafe and would be happy to tie the noose around her scrawny little neck.

Ignoring her suggestion, he redoubled his efforts to get her out. The only thing he could do to help her now would be to get her safely to her mother's folks on the reservation and hope the posse didn't track them.

"Let's try once more. Ready?"

"I guess. But take it easy on the...chest, okay?" Her voice was thin, wavery, like she'd all but given up hope.

That she'd overtly mentioned her, er, private areas, was proof positive that she was suffering from some sort of shock. Which was probably why she was showing so little faith in his ability. Unaccountably spurred by her distrust, Jericho bunched his muscles and jerked with all his might. The rope snapped tightly and he felt her body raise a full foot. Eight more to the edge of the pit.

By continually tightening the length of hemp around the post, he was able to secure the progress they'd made, and fifteen minutes later, her dark hair appeared over the lip of the pit. Jericho strained to hold the rope taut with his left hand while he fashioned a double-hitch knot around the post with his right. Sweat dripped in rapidly flowing rivers down his face by the time he finally gripped her wrists and pulled her to safety.

She was no sooner on her feet than she threw her arms around his neck and hugged him so tightly Jericho thought she just might slip inside his skin. His face was buried in her great dark cloud of hair and he was surprised at how soft, how oddly fragrant it was. Verity normally kept her ebony mane in a single braid down her back; he'd never really noticed its silky texture before.

In fact, there were several things he'd never noticed about Verity McBride. Jericho had always thought of her as a girl; he knew she was only eighteen or so. But the warm, supple body pressed against his was that of a woman. A full-bodied woman. With pillowy soft breasts pushing with gentle insistence against his chest.

He gulped and leaned backward, deliberately disengaging himself in hopes of breaking that surge of heat rising from his groin. Jericho Jackson might be the scalawag most decent folks thought him to be, but he didn't lust after young girls. Especially not the young daughter of a woman he called a friend.

But she smelled so damned enticing!

Placing his hands on her shoulders, he held her at arm's length, maintaining a gentlemanly distance between them. "Think you're okay to ride?"

As if sensing his discomfort, she took a step backward and said hesitantly, "I'm sorry. I was just so damned glad to be out of that pit!"

Although surprised by her casual use of a swear

word, he patted her shoulder, chagrined that he'd pushed her away when she was only expressing her gratitude. The poor kid hadn't had much affection in her life. Which reminded him that her life was apt to be a short one if he didn't get her away from Jerome before the law tracked her down. "I'm just glad you weren't hurt. Feel up to riding?"

"I feel up to riding to Panama, if you'll get me out of this mine."

He started to unravel her from the loop of rope when he noticed she was wrapped in a thick quilt. "What in the world are you wearing?"

"Oh, this must have been in the shaft. Good thing...I was freezing."

Jericho retrieved the kerosene lantern from the nail and stared at the faded quilt. It was a Seven Sisters design; he remembered watching Min-e-wah stitch the intricate pattern while she was in the family way with one of the boys. Even recalled that bit of bright red coming from an old vest he'd given Min-e-wah. The quilt had been a Christmas gift for Verity, but now the girl didn't even recognize it.

He swung the lantern up and studied her face. Her eyes looked clear and focused. Other than that, Jericho had no idea how to figure out the severity of a head injury. It was risky, but maybe he should try to sneak her into town and see Doc Greavy before taking her to her mother's tribe. He'd never forgive himself if something happened to Min-e-wah's daughter while she was entrusted to his care.

Nodding at the quilt, he said, "Hold that thing up so you don't trip on it. And stay right on my heels."

They'd only taken a couple steps when she called out, "I never did thank you properly, Mr...."

"Jackson. Jericho Jackson," he said automatically, then stopped abruptly and whirled to face her. "You don't remember my *name?*"

She frowned and slowly shook her head. "Your name *is* familiar, though I don't believe we've met."

Was she pulling his leg? She should know his name almost as well as her own. Years before, Min-e-wah had nursed him back to life after he'd been almost killed by a javelina. The wild boar had charged him from behind, breaking several ribs in the initial attack before butting, stomping and biting him until Jericho had somehow managed to cock his pistol and shoot the crazed animal. Min-e-wah found him two days later, wracked with fever and almost dead from the lack of water.

After that, Jericho had become almost like a brother to the lovely Apache widow and her half-white child. He'd cautioned her against marrying Rafe Wilson but Min-e-wah wanted her daughter raised in the white man's world. Rafe was a mean drunkard, but after Jericho had whipped his cowardly butt for beating his wife, there'd been no more incidents of violence. At least, none had been reported to Jericho.

But now Verity was staring at him with the eyes of a stranger.

He reached out and ran a fingertip over her soft, grimy cheek. "It's not important, Ver. Come on, let's get you out of here."

WHEN THEY FINALLY EMERGED from the mine entrance, Vera was startled to discover darkness had fallen. The tour bus had reached the Balbriggan around ten-thirty that morning. Granted, dusk came early in the winter, but still, she must have lain, unconscious, in that pit for several hours. Vera shuddered, faced with the grim reminder that she nearly lost her life in the fall.

Incredibly, snow had fallen sometime while she was trapped inside. The guide had warned them about rapid weather changes. Now the ground was covered with a thin layer of crunchy white. She was doubly glad she'd held on to the quilt while Mr. Jackson was towing her to safety. Vera remembered she'd left her jeans jacket in the tour van, and glanced at the spot where they'd parked the van. Empty. Not even a bare patch of ground in the snow. It was as if the van never existed.

Halting abruptly, she glanced around. Something was wrong; terribly wrong. There were no rescue vehicles, ambulances, patrol cars or helicopters. No flashing blue lights, no stretcher or any other sign of an organized rescue. If Jericho Jackson had driven his personal vehicle, it, too, was missing. Only a pair of horses were tied to a post near the mine entrance.

Suddenly, she wished she'd been able to bring her service revolver with her. She felt naked without its comforting and equalizing weight.

Bewildered and slightly frightened, she turned to Jericho. "Wh-where's the rescue rig? And the paramedics?"

"What are paramedics?" he asked after a long pause.

"Maybe you call them something else around here, EMTs or medics."

"EMTs?"

She waved an impatient hand. "Emergency Medical Technicians, or something like that. Where's your unit? I don't understand, why are you here all alone?"

Another long pause. "Because your message specifically said for me to come alone. Because of Rafe."

"Rafe?"

"Yeah, some folks are taking his death kind of hard. Especially him being killed by an Indian."

Vera tossed her head, to clear the cobwebs so she could try to make sense of his words. What on earth did she have to do with some man who was killed by an Indian? And why did Jackson keep referring to some message she supposedly sent?

Had those blows to her head caused her to have some kind of amnesia? Vera didn't think so because she could clearly remember every detail up until the time the rotted board broke and plunged her headlong down that mine shaft.

Maybe she'd talked with him when she was only half conscious. That must be it; he was referring to some conversation they'd had when she was only semiconscious. She'd go back to the hotel, get a good night's sleep and it would all be clear in the morning.

Lifting her chin, she noted the look of concern on his rugged face. Nice face, actually. Lean, lots of angles and a neatly trimmed mustache. Maybe not a luxuriant Sam Elliott mustache, but sexy nonetheless. She shrugged her shoulders and grinned. "I must have bonked my head pretty hard. Eight hours on a soft pillow and I'll be good as new. So, where's your car?''

Jericho shook his head, and stared hard into her eyes. Even though she could barely see his eyes in the dim light cast by his lantern, she could make out the confusion and worry. ''My car?''

''Or truck, or whatever you drive.''

He shook his head, looking as awestruck as a first-grader trying to make sense of Einstein's theory of relativity. Unless Vera was badly mistaken, he didn't have a clue what she was talking about. They were having a serious breakdown in communication here. The wind was blowing frigid gusts down her back, she was exhausted and wanted nothing more than to slide between a pair of crisp white sheets.

Drawing on an almost empty reserve of patience, she tried again. ''Inside you asked if I was ready to ride. So I'm asking, ride in what? Where did you park?''

He hitched a thumb toward the horses. ''Over there.''

''A horse! You expect me to ride ten miles into town, in a snowstorm, on horseback?''

Her tone brought him out of his apparent stupor. ''I'm damn sure not going to carry you piggyback, Verity. Now let's quit jawing and get going. We've got a long ride, because we can't use the main road.''

''Why on earth not?'' She wrapped the quilt tighter around her shoulders. None of this was making any sense. And his peculiar behavior was starting to frighten her. She wasn't about to go off on any side roads with this odd stranger.

After a long, tense, pause, he said softly, "Verity, we need to get you to Doc Greavy's right away. I don't know what's happened to you here, but something's dreadful wrong."

"You got that right, but *I'm* not the one with the problem. And stop calling me Verity, it gives me the creeps. My name is Vera."

He took off his black hat and pushed his fingers through a thick patch of equally dark hair. "I'll call you any damn thing you want if you'll get on that horse over there."

Her head swiveled to follow his pointing finger. "Is that the only way into town?"

He shrugged. "Unless you want to walk."

Vera considered her options. She could either mount a horse, which she'd never done in her life, and go off into the night with this very strange man, or she could try to walk ten miles through heavy snow into Jerome. Or she could wait here and hope that help arrived before she froze to death.

Marching through the packed snow, she cautiously approached the animals. "Do they bite?"

SILENTLY, THEY COVERED the two winding miles down the side of the mountain. Jericho was still pondering her strange behavior. Verity McBride had almost been *born* in a saddle; he knew for a fact she was a skilled horsewoman by her tenth birthday. But tonight she acted as if she'd never *seen* a horse before. He'd had to coach her on mounting, tell her how to hold the reins, and how to nudge the horse's side with her foot, all the while constantly reassuring her that her own horse wouldn't harm her!

And those funny shoes she was wearing. Jericho had never seen anything like them. Pure white leather except for some purple swirl across the heel. And short rubber soles. Ugly and not very practical. You needed a thick sturdy heel to grip the stirrup, and high leather boots to protect your legs from burrs and chaparral.

When they reached the bottom of the mountain, she didn't argue when he headed them toward the narrow mine road into town, instead of the coach road. He kept glancing behind, keeping a wary eye on her. She looked so forlorn, huddled in that quilt, as if she were lost and didn't have a friend in the world. Well, she wasn't so far wrong at that.

When Rafe Wilson's body was found with a single bullet wound in his back, folks had gotten riled about him being killed by a coward. Not many were actually grieving for Rafe, being the no-account drunk that he was, but the hardy townspeople didn't much cotton to killing a man from behind.

The original speculation was that he'd been caught cheating at cards; Rafe was known for lending fate a hand from time to time.

But then the oldest Wilson boy had rushed into the saloon looking for Jericho, who was…indisposed over at Rosie's Sporting House for a couple hours. The frightened boy blurted out his news that had spread like wildfire; Verity McBride had killed her pa for smacking her mother. The hot-blooded miners had reacted immediately; Rafe Wilson might have been an SOB, but he didn't deserve to be shot in the back. And certainly not by his half-breed stepdaughter.

In moments, the grumbling drinkers had turned into a lynch mob. Right now, they were prowling through the high desert area between town and Rafe Wilson's shack. They wouldn't waste any time stringing Verity from the nearest tree if they found her.

But before Jericho could sneak her down to the Apache encampment, he had to get her to Doc Greavy's. It was obvious to Jericho that, at best, the girl had gone loco; at worst, she might be dying.

Chapter Three

The sun rose, a bright golden orb peeking over the edge of the mountains, bringing much needed warmth. During the long, silent night, Vera had remained grateful for the cushioning warmth of the quilt. But she was as confused as ever about the sequence of events that led to her rescue the night before.

After riding for what felt like hours, Jericho had finally relented enough to allow a brief respite. Vera felt she'd no sooner fallen asleep than Jericho's booted foot nudged her awake. Without so much as a cup of bracing coffee, they remounted.

Jericho rode almost silently, only occasionally pointing out a potential pitfall. He hadn't uttered a single conversational word since they'd mounted up outside the mine.

Vera shifted in the saddle for the thousandth time in the past hour. The pain in her backside had passed sore, gone beyond miserable, and was well on the way to agony, but she didn't complain for fear the strange man leading the way might just go off and leave her alone in the wilderness.

Suddenly, he stopped and turned, pressing his index finger to his lips. "Shhh. Don't make a sound."

Slipping off his own horse, he led hers behind a large boulder and helped her dismount. Rubbing her weary rump, she started to ask what was wrong when he shook his head. "Shhh. Wait here."

He handed her the reins and, taking off his black broad-brimmed hat, stole back around to the other side of the sandstone boulder. In a few seconds, he tiptoed back and said in a hushed voice, "About nine of them, but I think they'll pass us by."

"Nine of whom?" she whispered.

"Lawmen."

"Good! Maybe they can—" She broke off when he cupped a hand over her mouth.

"Don't talk so loud!" He cast an anxious glance over his shoulder. "You know how sound carries out here."

Finally, he pulled his hand away, but the warm imprint tingled on her face for long seconds afterward. Making sure to keep her tone barely audible, she cautiously probed, "But aren't they looking for us?"

"Yeah, they're on your trail."

"Then why don't we just let them know where we are?"

His dark eyes blinked rapidly as he patted her hand, an oddly pitying gesture. "Verity—Vera, sugar, you're going to have to trust me here. Seems like you don't recall much about what's happening, and I hate to be the one to bring unwelcome news, but...but those men want to hang you."

"What! You must be joking."

"I'm afraid not. Now, please, keep your voice down."

Stunned silent, Vera leaned against the rock, certain she'd collapse if not for its cold support. Everything around her was off-kilter, askew, as though she'd strayed into the fun house at the carnival and was hopelessly lost in the bizarre darkness. "B-but why would they want to arrest me? I mean, I didn't even know they still hung people, but what is it they think I've done?"

"Murder."

A cold chill washed through her like someone had poured a bucket of ice water down her throat. "This is crazy, Jericho! I haven't killed anyone, and I certainly haven't been tried and convicted."

"And if Jess Wiggins and that bunch have their way, there won't be a trial."

Vera's head started pounding again, and she unconsciously raised her hands to rub her temples. Weary beyond belief, she tried to make sense of his dire words. "Mr. Jackson, I can't imagine what you're talking about. Who is it I'm supposed to have killed?"

"Rafe, as if you didn't already know. Course, it's a pure miracle to me that somebody didn't plug the old bastard long before now. But you know how they feel in these parts about...well, about you being part Indian."

A fresh wave of dizziness washed over her, adding to the throbbing in her temples. What did the trace of Indian blood she carried have to do with anything?

Who was Rafe and why would anyone imagine she'd killed him?

Suddenly, she remembered leaving the rental car keys on the dresser at the motel. Maybe someone had stolen her car and this Rafe person had been killed in a hit-and-run. And if the plates were traced to the rental company, then, of course, she would be implicated. It had to be something like that. Something easily explainable. If she could get to town and speak to the authorities...

"Mr. Jackson, please listen to me. I'm a CHP officer from California. I didn't kill that man, or anyone else. I can show the deputies my badge—they can easily verify my credentials. The accident can easily be explained if I—"

He snorted. "I don't rightly know how you can accidentally shoot someone in the back, but I'm willing to listen. Unlike those men down there."

"Shot in the back! This doesn't make any sense."

Vera stared hard at Jericho who was watching her closely, a nervous look on his handsome face. What did she really know about him? So far, she had only his word that she was wanted by the law. Was he inventing this horrible story to instill fear in hopes of keeping her under his control?

Closing her eyes, she tried to remember everything she'd ever heard about stalkers and serial killers. Someday, if the hiring freeze ever lifted, she intended to transfer to the San Francisco PD. Although her investigative skills weren't utilized very much in her CHP duties, she still attended seminars and read a great deal of law enforcement literature to keep her knowledge current. And her training offered a great deal of insight into the serial killer mentality. They liked their victims meek, yielding. Frightened and feeling helpless. Well, that's the last face she'd present to Jericho Jackson—if that was even his real name.

Straightening up, she forced a steely edge into her voice. "This has to be some kind of sick joke, and I want you to stop right now."

A flash of empathy shone in his dark eyes, before he quickly looked away, avoiding her beseeching gaze. "I wish to God I had the power to do just that. For your mother's sake, if for no other reason."

"My mother! You—you knew my mother?" The moment she blurted out her question, she regretted showing him even a momentary weakness. Everyone had a mother; it took no great wisdom to realize that referring to her mother would evoke strong emotion. She had to remember to act cool, in control. "Stop lying to me! You don't know me or anyone in my family."

He jerked around to face her. "I said keep your voice down!" Crouching low to the ground, he eased around the side of the boulder and watched the horseback riders who were now trailing away like a stream of hungry ants. "I don't think they heard you, but it might be a trick. They might go around that bend and double back. We'd better hurry."

He rose to his feet, as smooth and fluid as a puma preparing to pounce and started for his horse.

The quilt sliding unnoticed onto the ground, Vera quickly scrambled to her feet and grabbed his woolen sleeve. "I'm not moving a muscle until you tell me the truth."

She planted her feet and crossed her arms, partly for effect and partly to ward off the brisk chill penetrating her thin chambray shirt. She only wished she felt as confident as her stance would lead him to believe. During the course of her career, Vera had held her own against a number of mentally disturbed individuals and armed felons. But now, without the equalizing implements of side arm, baton and Taser, Vera was unarmed and largely defenseless.

Jericho cocked his hat with his thumb, flapped his arms a couple of times in obvious exasperation, then stalked over to stand in front of her. Uncomfortably close. Despite her best intentions, Vera took an involuntary step backward.

Lifting her eyes to meet his, she stood in apparent calm, waiting for his response. She didn't have long to wait.

Speaking between tightly clenched teeth, he muttered, "I realize you're not thinking too clearly on account of that fall. But we don't have time to dwell on this, Verity, you've got to—"

"Hold it right there!" she interrupted. "Why do you keep calling me by that name?"

"Because it's yours."

She tossed her head in frustration and poked her own chest for emphasis. "*I'm* not the one who's confused, Mr. Jackson. Verity McBride is the girl your local legend is built around. *I'm* Vera McBride—an extremely distant relative of Verity, that's true, but

I'm a bit younger. In case you hadn't noticed." *About a century younger.*

"Oh, I noticed all right. A man would have to be blind not to notice your...attractions." He cast a blatantly appraising look along the length of her body, pausing to stare at her cold-hardened nipples prodding the thin chambray fabric. "But younger? The Verity I know is a gawkish girl, but you, Miss Vera McBride, are most definitely a full-grown woman."

Vera held a hand to her head, which was whirling in confusion. What kind of sick game was he playing? The way he kept talking as if he knew Verity, when the girl disappeared decades before he was even born.

Fear clenched like a tight fist in her stomach. Obviously Jericho Jackson, sexy though he might be, was...mentally unhinged. He was no more a part of a search-and-rescue effort than she was. Somehow he'd stumbled into the mine, and for that she should be grateful. But he was so strange, so unpredictable, that Vera wouldn't feel truly safe until she was well away from him.

"Mr. Jackson, I simply can't argue any longer. Just take me into town and I'll see that you're amply rewarded for your efforts."

He grinned and tossed his head. "Not so fast, Miss *Vera* McBride. We never finished our discussion. So you're a distant relative who just happened to be holed up in the very mine where *Verity* asked me to meet her? I'd say that was a powerful coincidence, wouldn't you?"

Sorry she'd ever begun this conversation, Vera chewed her bottom lip and considered his strange demeanor. Obviously he believed she was some kind of…reincarnation…of Verity McBride. Which at least explained the murder charge she was supposed to be fleeing.

Maybe if she blurted out the truth he'd snap back into some kind of awareness; she'd heard of people who drifted in and out of derangement. And he seemed to have at least a few periods of relative lucidity. "Mr. Jackson, I don't know who Verity McBride asked or didn't ask to meet her before she disappeared. But that was over a hundred years ago!"

He bucked backward and roared, his unexpected laughter loud and disconcerting in the silent dawn before he abruptly choked it off. "Your mother always said you had a knack for weaving tall tales. That one ought to be written up in a penny dreadful."

He reached out and roughly grasped her shoulders. "Now you listen to me, sugar. This is no time to be funning around—that posse is hot for the smell of your blood. I owe your mother, and I'll be damned if I'll let 'em hang her daughter. But I'm not anxious to get strung up beside you. Now quit this nonsense and let's get going."

Vera had been willing to concede to anything just to get him to lead her into Jerome. Until he'd called her sugar. Now she wanted nothing more than to raise this pseudocowpoke's social consciousness a notch or two. "I don't know what you good ole boys get away with around here, Mr. Jackson, but with the millennium approaching most men have outgrown the caveman tactics."

His head reared back. "Beg your pardon?"

Vera counted ten, and kept reminding herself that the man she was dealing with was obviously a few spokes short of a wheel. "I'm saying, Mr. Jackson, that men don't call women sugar anymore."

He shook his dark head. "No. The other part. About the milli-something."

"The millennium. The twenty-first century, 2001."

"2001?" His voice was suddenly weak, barely audible. "You're talking about the year 2001, is that right?"

"Of course. Everyone is looking forward to the new century. With the scientific evidence recently uncovered, maybe they'll discover life exists on Mars after all."

He slumped against the boulder and washed his face with his palms. Drawing a deep breath, he stood up again. "Miss *Vera*…er, is *Miss* all right?"

"It'll do, but I prefer Ms."

"Uh-huh." He fingered his mustache thoughtfully. "Well, ma'am, I'm truly hornswoggled here. Exactly what date do you think this is?"

Vera rolled her eyes. December eleventh wasn't it, when she'd gone into the mine? And they'd ridden through the rest of the night. "Today must be the twelfth."

His eyes lit up in obvious surprise. "That's right! December 12, 1896."

Glad they'd finally reached an agreement, Vera had bent over to pick up her quilt when his words finally struck home. She straightened slowly and turned to face him once more. "Mr. Jackson, did you say *1896?*"

That wary look crept back on his face. "Sure. I've owned the saloon almost two years now. Remember when I opened? New Year's Eve, 1894. You were just a young gal but you must remember that big party we threw? Everybody in town came."

When she didn't respond, he reached over and tipped up her chin until their faces were scant inches apart. "Come on, Verity, the game's over. You're starting to spook me...what's wrong?"

She sank to the ground and hugged her knees against her chest. A sick, horrible certainty was boiling in the pit of her stomach. Jericho Jackson wasn't just a little "off." He was a complete lunatic. One who thought he was living over a hundred years in the past.

Because he'd deliberately steered them away from the main highway, Vera had no idea how to get back to Jerome. Even in December, the harsh landscape could be lethal. Winter storms or unseasonal hot spells were equally possible. Heatstroke, snakebite, scorpions and freezing nights lay in wait for the inexperienced traveler in this unfamiliar and hostile land.

She had to stay with him until they reached civilization. No matter what it took, she had to play along and not let him see her fear. Humor him. Get to safety. Then run like hell and never look back.

Looking up, she shielded her eyes against the bright sun that was rapidly moving higher in the sky. "How much farther to Jerome, Mr. Jackson?"

"About two miles," he said as he untied the reins

and led the horses toward her. She noticed he didn't obligingly indicate which direction.

Still shaky, but determined to outwit him somehow, she rose to her feet and draped the folded quilt across the saddle. Maybe the additional padding would offer some relief for her aching rear. Hitching her backpack onto her shoulders, she drew a deep fortifying breath and approached the chestnut mare.

Jericho laced his fingers and Vera stepped into his hands and hoisted herself up onto the smaller horse. When he'd mounted, she softly clicked her tongue to urge the horse, but Jericho stayed her hand with his. "We'd better head back the other way."

Filled with a sudden sense of dread, she whispered, "Why?"

For an answer, he raised his arm and pointed at the valley below, where they'd last seen the band of riders.

Vera's gaze followed the course of his finger. At first all she could see was a cloud of dust, building and swirling like a mini tornado sweeping through the dry valley. After a moment, however, she could pick out figures in the midst of that brown cloud. Nine men on horseback. Riding hard. Right toward them.

GRABBING THE REINS from her hand, Jericho swung around and started back the way they'd come. He forced a more rapid pace than they'd previously traveled and, despite the quilt's extra padding, Vera's tender bottom thumped painfully on the leather saddle.

About a mile back up the path, he took a sudden

detour to the right and pointed to a steep, narrow trail leading down the mountain. "Didn't want to take Dead Man's Trail with you so shaky and all, but...now we don't have a choice."

Vera understood perfectly. In his mind, she was Verity McBride and if they didn't evade the encroaching vigilantes, she would be captured, or worse, hanged. While Vera would rather take her chances with the nine riders, she knew Jericho would never be persuaded to wait.

His apprehension was palpable in the still mountain air and she wondered for the first time who those men really were. If they weren't chasing her, who *were* they after? A certain lanky cowboy in a long black coat and black Stetson? She had a sudden clear recollection of old cowboy movies on TV; the bad guys *always* wore black.

Taking her silence for assent, Jericho tied the reins of her horse to his saddle and they began picking their way down the treacherous trail.

After a single, horrifying glance over the edge, Vera kept her eyes focused straight ahead. In that one quick look, she'd estimated the bottom to be over a thousand feet below. Jericho, she noted, kept casting anxious glances over his shoulder as if he expected the riders to appear behind them at any moment.

As they continued their slow descent, the path steepened so sharply that a single misstep would plunge them over the precipice. To quell the terror that mounted with each crunch of hooves on the rock-strewn trail, Vera thought about the men following them. They had to be after Jericho. What had he done that they pursued him so intently, with such determination?

The full extent of her predicament started to sink in and her stomach lurched with the unwelcome realization. Jericho hadn't saved her out of the goodness of his heart; maybe he'd seen an opportunity to acquire a hostage. By tying her reins to his saddle, he insured she couldn't escape. But at his own peril. If one of them went over the cliff, the other would surely follow. A man that desperate wouldn't hesitate to trade her life for his.

Yet what could she do but follow blindly, while hoping and praying for an opportunity to flee?

All her experience and training urged her to tread carefully. Pretend to believe his fantastic claims and bide her time until the odds of escape swung in her favor. She'd never felt so helpless, so vulnerable in her life and didn't care for the feeling one bit.

It took well over an hour to traverse down Dead Man's Trail. When they finally, thankfully, reached the dry riverbed at the bottom, Vera started to shake with relief from the sustained tension.

Jericho paused and waited until she drew up beside him. He unhitched her reins and tossed them back to her. "The worst is over," he said with a trace of compassion in his voice. The inadvertent show of kindness was cut out quickly when his voice hardened once more. "You ought to be able to manage from here on in."

Sure, now that they'd left the lawmen far behind. No danger letting her have control of her horse now.

Vera said nothing.

He reached behind his bedroll and held up a canteen. "Thirsty?"

She licked her parched lips and nodded. He might be the devil in black denim, but right now she'd sell her soul for a drink of anything—even devil's brew.

He handed her the canteen and she sipped the tepid, brackish water. "Ugh."

"Sorry about that," he said with an insincere grin. "Didn't have time to empty the old water out and refill it before taking off after you, er, Verity."

Vera wished he'd stop this mindless game and just tell her the truth; that he was wanted by the law and had taken her hostage to guarantee his freedom. But for now she kept her silence. This sliver of knowledge allowed her to stay one step ahead of him. She had to make him believe she accepted his silly charade of benign insanity.

When she'd had her fill, she handed him back the canteen and watched as he tipped his head back and drained it. His unfathomable face was all hard edges and rough planes. Thick eyebrows that shadowed his eyes, a strong, forceful chin and firmly defined jawline. Darkly, coldly handsome. Only the occasional glimpse of light behind his charcoal eyes gave him humanity. And his incongruously soft mouth.

Yet behind that roughly pleasing facade possibly lurked a cold-blooded killer. And she couldn't forget that for a single moment. Maybe *he'd* shot a man in the back....

He glanced up at the sun which was moving ever higher in the sky and nodded. "Enough rest. Let's finish this."

Vera deliberately closed her mind against the vivid imaginings of exactly how he intended to "finish" with her. Sucking her bottom lip between her teeth, she tapped the horse's belly with her heel and followed Jericho.

After a short, uneventful ride, they rounded a curve at the base of the mountain. Jericho drew up his horse and pointed. The ramshackle shantytown of Jerome was dead ahead. She'd made it! Although she wasn't much of a rider, surely she could make it into town and find the police before Jericho could catch her. Safety was in sight.

"Damn, that sun's hot," Jericho declared as he pulled off his black canvas slicker.

That was when Vera first noticed the gun belt strapped around his hips. Her heart sank. She'd have to let him play out his hand, whatever it was. While she *might* be able to elude him on horseback, she wasn't foolish enough to think she could outrun a bullet.

She knuckled back a tear of frustration and tipped up her chin. He would never see her fear. Nor realize her overwhelming sense of helplessness. Not if she could help it.

Once again Jericho took the lead as they slowly rode up the dusty road into the vertically constructed town that reminded her of a Tinkertoy village perched on the mountainside. The narrow roads—

Vera's breath caught. The roads had been paved, hadn't they? Now they were mostly dirt with cobblestone patches scattered here and there.

An eerie feeling seeped into her bones and she felt chilled despite the sun's warmth. Everything looked the same, yet somehow different. The rickety wooden structures looked faded and devoid of charm. Funny, until today she'd thought the brightly painted gift shops and restaurants were picturesque and inviting.

Now Jerome looked like the stage set of an old western movie.

Ah, she thought. Movie magic. "When did the film crew come in?" she asked conversationally. "It's amazing what they can do in a few short hours."

He drew up and stared at her. "Film? Movies? What kind of jabber is that? Something else they do in the California of your dreams?"

"But yesterday, there were cars and telephone poles and..." Her voice trailed off as he continued to stare at her face. Complete bewilderment mingled with a strange sadness in his eyes.

He flicked the reins and they started moving down the dusty road once more. Vera's head swiveled from side to side as she tried to understand the incomprehensible changes since yesterday.

There were no pedestrians strolling along the wooden sidewalks, but that in itself wasn't surprising. It was too early for tourists and the town was mainly a tourist attraction with few full-time residents. Nor was the absence of cars disturbing. Because the streets were so narrow, parking was mostly confined to a couple of public lots at the far end of town.

But there was a strange...smell floating over the small village. Not at all reminiscent of the aroma of Mrs. Beasley's fresh apple pies that had previously emanated from her small bakery.

Vera stopped and stared, not sure what she was looking for. "What's that odd smell?" she asked.

Jericho cocked his head. "You mean the copper smelter?"

She swung around and stared at his ingenuous face. "But I thought the mines were all closed down."

He laughed. "I don't know where you'd get that idea. If the mines closed, this place would become a ghost town overnight."

Exactly, she thought. From her readings, Vera knew mining had hit its heyday in Jerome in the late 1880s, then again during World War I when copper went up as high as thirty cents a pound. But the industry never quite recovered from the stock market crash of 1929.

When the mines finally ceased operation in the 1950s, the locals had quickly fled to the valley for the few available jobs. Jerome had been a virtual ghost town for years before a few poor artists migrated to the hillside community and claimed it. Then it was an impromptu artists' colony until tourism picked up about fifteen years before.

After that brief, largely unprofitable, flurry of mining activity in the fifties, the smelter had been closed for decades. Yet this morning the unmistakably acrid scent of copper fouled the air.

Down the street a door creaked open and a young boy drifted outside. "The town's starting to come alive," Jericho murmured. "We'd better get you out of sight."

He stopped in front of the Gilbert Hotel and hitched their horses to the wooden post. Reaching up, he held out his arms and Vera obligingly placed her hands on his strong shoulders and allowed him to help her alight.

"Come on, Doc Greavy's office is around the corner, remember?"

No, she didn't remember and for the first time in

her life Vera started to doubt her own sanity. The little boy who'd ventured outdoors was garbed in baggy brown trousers held up by suspenders. He carried a stick and a large hoop. An antique toy. The kind children played with in the late 1800s.

A door opened and another boy ran out to join him. He, too, was dressed in the same peculiar clothing as the first.

Jericho Jackson's insane fantasies aside, there had to be a logical explanation for all these changes. She stopped the boy when he skipped by.

"Excuse me, boys! Would you come here for a minute, please?"

They stopped and stared quizzically at her jeans and sneakers. "Yes, ma'am?"

"Would you answer a question for me?"

The first boy, obviously the braver of the pair, stepped forward. "I will if I can."

Question, question. What could she ask him that would prove once and for all that she wasn't in the Twilight Zone?

"Who's the president? Of the United States?"

He laughed and nudged his buddy. "Don't you know, ma'am?"

"Yes, but my friend and I are having a little bet."

The boys understood betting. The second youngster inched up to stand beside his friend. "We just had an election. You want the name of the man going out or coming into office?"

"Both."

Enjoying this silly adult game, the boys shrugged. The boy with the hoop ultimately answered. "Mr. Cleveland's stepping down and Mr. William McKinley from Ohio will be the new president. Did you win, ma'am?''

"Yes," she said faintly. "I won."

The boys rolled the hoop down the street and Vera, her mind fogged in disbelief, stared after them.

She suddenly recalled Jericho's shock when she hadn't recognized him. Her mind, still foggy from her fall, hadn't made the connection. But Verity had often mentioned a Jericho Jackson in her journal. And a Rafe! Verity's stepfather.

Feeling dazed and uncertain, Vera took small, unwilling steps down the planked sidewalk. On the corner, exactly where the Blue Bonnet Café had been located the day before, a sign now proclaimed the building to be the *Jerome Sentinel*. The newspaper. But hadn't someone told her that Jerome no longer had a local paper?

Frowning, she stepped closer to the plate glass window where the latest edition was displayed. In a bold, ornate typeface, the headline proclaimed, "Local Girl Sought In Murder!"

A fuzzy photo below the caption chilled Vera's blood in her veins. The hair was different and the cheekbones were a bit higher, more prominent, but the girl in the newspaper was a dead ringer for Vera.

Almost against her will, Vera's eyes trailed upward, to the date. December 12, 1896.

For the first time in her life, she fainted.

Chapter Four

Jericho was so stunned he barely caught the woman before her head slammed into the hard-packed earth. Verity was obviously in worse health than he'd credited, to faint dead away like that. No woman could survive years of living with a miserable scum-licker like Rafe Wilson without becoming a bit hardened. But this recent trouble seemed to have penetrated her hard shell; softened her.

Her momentary weakness, even if it was based on her injuries, made him feel protective. And oddly proud. As if she'd trusted him enough not to take advantage of her unguarded moment of vulnerability.

For the second time in less than a day, Jericho lifted the soft woman into his arms. Now what? She was light enough, but he wasn't going to risk trundling her up that narrow, rickety flight of stairs to Doc Greavy's office. And he couldn't leave her on the ground like an abandoned puppy. If any of the newly commissioned posse spotted her, Verity's, er, Vera's, life span wouldn't be long enough to bother fetching the doctor.

With a growl of frustration, he carried his unconscious bundle around the corner into the alley. Rich, red dollops of mud slathered Jericho's black boots with each forceful stride, but he scarcely noticed. His attention was focused on the still alley, as he watched for any unexpected movement. When he was finally convinced the narrow walkway was clear of onlookers, he looked around for a safe place to hide his charge while he went for the doctor.

A handcart was parked outside the hotel's back door, a stained canvas tarp concealing its load.

Jericho propped his foot against the cart wheel for balance and shifted the woman's dead weight against his body, freeing his right arm. Raising the edge of the tarp, he glanced inside at a pile of fresh-smelling hay. Perfect. He yanked the covering aside and deftly lifted the woman's sleeping form over the wooden lip and lowered her into the hay pile.

She stirred and moaned softly in her sleep. He fingered aside a strand of silky black hair from her eyes, startled at the softness of her skin. Few women of his acquaintance had skin as soft as rose petals. Too little water and too few comforts tanned the flesh of most frontier women into leather before their twentieth birthday. Yet "Vera's" cheek was as soft and supple as that of an infant. This strangely unfamiliar woman was turning into an intriguing source of unending surprise.

Jericho scanned the alley once more before loosely slipping the canvas back over the cart, leaving an open edge so air could circulate. He knew the hotel housekeeper would use the straw to freshen the bed pillows when she cleaned the rooms. With any luck she wouldn't get to that chore until her breakfast duties were finished; that cart should remain undisturbed for several hours yet.

Taking another surreptitious glance around to satisfy himself that his actions had gone unnoticed, Jericho whistled softly as he strode down the muddy alleyway to the doctor's office.

VERA COULDN'T REMEMBER ever being so tired. She wanted nothing more than to nestle deeper into the covers and sleep the morning away. But something kept poking into her cheek.

Half asleep, she reached up and plucked away the offending straw. A blade of grass? In her bed?

Her eyes fluttered open. She was startled to discover it was still dark. She reached for the bedside lamp, but her searching hand encountered a wooden board of some kind blocking the bed. Confused, she reached out to the other side and gasped. Another wooden board. She was crated up as if...as if she were in a coffin.

Panic seeping into her bones, Vera tried to sit up but her head encountered a third obstacle. For a moment, she feared she truly had been buried alive but reason took control when she realized the top covering was flexible. Pushing aside the heavy material, she sat up and looked around. The sight of Jericho Jackson, long black coat flapping around his long black-clad legs, brought her predicament back into sharp focus.

And the astounding conclusion she'd reached to explain this inexplicable situation. Unless she had completely slipped off the trolley track, in which case she should be institutionalized for her own safety, Vera believed that she'd somehow traveled through time and landed in 1896.

She laughed, a nervous, frightened chortle that had nothing to do with humor. The entire idea was ridiculous, and yet…Vera was scared. As frightened as she'd ever been in her life. No bogeyman, no nighttime monster could compare with this sense of being caught out of her own time. As she thought over all the tiny signs she'd noted and discarded, she became even more convinced that the impossible had happened.

She'd come to Arizona looking for Verity McBride, now somehow, she had become her own ancestor. At least, that's what Jericho seemed to think, and he'd known Verity well enough to recognize her on sight. But if some cosmic abberation had caused her to change places with a girl who'd disappeared over a hundred years earlier, why did she retain her own sense of awareness? Her own memories?

No, she hadn't traded places with her notorious ancestor, though she was being tracked like a wild animal for the other woman's alleged crime.

As Jericho drew nearer, a ferocious scowl on his face, she thought briefly of confiding her predicament and asking for his help. The idea fled as quickly as she'd conceived it. This man had never seen a car or a telephone, much less a computer. Giving women the vote would be a novel idea to him; how on earth could he absorb a complex theory like time travel? Vera wasn't sure she understood or believed it herself, and she was the one who'd been hurled into a parallel dimension.

For now, she'd best keep her mode of transportation to herself and find another way to enlist Jericho Jackson's help or she was liable to find herself hanging from a tree limb.

Forcing a smile onto her face, she said, "Guess I fainted. Sorry to be so much trouble."

Relief flared in his eyes. "No trouble. It's not uncommon for a lady to succumb to the vapors when she's distressed. By the way, when was the last time you had anything to eat?"

Oh, about a hundred years ago, she thought, wondering what his reaction would be if she blurted out the truth. *The vapors?* She ought to shake his world and tell him about the symptoms of PMS. Instead, she shrugged. "Actually, it's been quite a while since I ate. Do they serve breakfast at the hotel?"

"Yeah, but I don't reckon it's smart for you to appear in public right now. Best keep you out of sight at my place 'til the doc gets back from delivering Mrs. Nesbitt's latest little one."

"I really don't need a doctor. Food would be good though."

He thumbed up the rim of his cowboy hat. "Listen, Rafe Wilson was one of the most cussed, black-hearted, ground-slinking dogs around these parts, but folks don't take kindly to back-shooting. Unless you want to be guest of honor at a necktie party, you'd best let me tuck you away before somebody spots you."

Vera hesitated. Now that she was reasonably certain Jericho wasn't a madman or a serial killer, she didn't find the idea of relying on him as alarming as when she'd first met him. Nonetheless, she didn't know a thing about this taciturn man. He *said* Verity had sent a message to him; that would indicate the girl had trusted him. Yet Verity had disappeared without a trace. Had her faith in Jericho Jackson been betrayed?

Vera cast an appraising glance at his lean, sensually enticing face. Could she trust him? Did she really have any choice?

Vera didn't know another soul in this town, even in this century, and she couldn't risk turning herself into the authorities. Her options were few and imperative. Somehow, she must clear Verity's name and get these murder charges dropped. Only then could Vera hope to solve the riddle of how she'd come through time—and figure out how to get back.

Noting Jericho's impatient boot tapping, she raised a hand. "Okay, I give. Let's go to your house."

He lifted a quizzical eyebrow. "Room, actually," he replied as he easily hefted her out of the hay wagon. "I don't have a house, remember? Since I spend about twenty hours a day working, I appropriated a couple of rooms over the saloon for myself. Can you walk?"

"I...I think so." Obviously, he expected her to know his housing situation.

If she wanted to gain his trust she had to tread carefully, build on his belief that she was Verity. For she sensed he was willing to go to extreme measures to help the young fugitive.

To deflect his curiosity at her apparent memory lapse, she released the steadying influence of his arm and tested her legs. A bit wobbly but she could walk under her own steam—if Mr. Long Legs didn't keep up too fast a pace.

With Jericho's arm hovering near her waist, they traversed the few hundred feet to the back door of the Copper Penny with little problem. Holding her out of sight with his forearm, he opened the squeaky door and peeked inside. "Come on." He cocked his head. Taking her hand, he led the way inside.

Although he took her upstairs by way of a narrow back staircase, so that Vera didn't get a glimpse of the saloon itself, she was startled by the echoing silence of the cavernous building. "Where is everybody?" she instinctively whispered.

"Charlie's out front cleaning. I imagine most of the girls are still asleep."

Girls? Vera's step faltered. She'd somehow assumed the Copper Penny merely catered to the drinking and gambling needs of the miners; she'd never imagined that Jericho serviced their carnal needs as well. Glancing over her shoulder, she assessed him with a more discerning eye. Although his black garb was frosted with trail dust and thick red mud, the fabric was finely woven. The jacquard vest was brocaded with golden threads.

Was her fate tied to the Wild West version of a pimp? Did Jericho Jackson run a bawdy house? Alarm and...disappointment shuddered through her. If her fears turned out to be founded, Vera knew she'd have to relinquish Jericho's dubious protection. Even if a lynch mob was the alternative, she couldn't take refuge with a man who made a living off the degradation of women.

When they reached the second-floor landing, Jericho motioned for Vera to stay on the staircase while he eased into the hall. A moment later, he waggled a beckoning finger and she joined him.

They were at the end of a long hallway. The area was more like a gallery than the hallways of modern hotels. A half-dozen doors marched along one wall while a spindled railing on the opposite side guarded unwary guests from falling to the saloon floor below.

Edging to the railing, Vera glanced down. The barroom was almost stereotypical in its Old West atmosphere. A polished wooden bar dominated the room. Three green baize-topped tables stood against the wall opposite the bar and about a dozen battered wooden tables were scattered between, mismatched chairs neatly set beneath them. Instead of swinging louvered doors at the entrance, a pair of copper-faced doors, with frosted glass panes near the top, were closed against street traffic.

Jericho pointed to a second hallway, intersecting with the first. "Come on, this way."

Said the spider to the fly, Vera thought, wondering if he had plans to recruit her into his harem of soiled doves. Then, knowing she had no choice—at least for the moment, she followed him into the dim, cavelike darkness.

VERA PATTED her stomach and leaned back in the chair, surveying the meager remains of the huge breakfast she'd just devoured. Steak, served with three eggs, a mound of fried potatoes, and warm, homemade bread slathered with fresh butter. No wonder photos of old west women portrayed them as...fleshy, she thought. A couple more meals of these gargantuan proportions and she'd have to trade her jeans for that heavy spread draping Jericho's bed.

Moving to the narrow window overlooking the street, she fingered aside the lace curtains and studied the now bustling roadway. Reminiscent of a scene from an early John Wayne movie, the eerily familiar tableau played out before her disbelieving eyes. Suspendered men loaded buckboards with feed sacks and rough bales of hay, and calico-dressed women dragged recalcitrant youngsters along the uneven wooden sidewalk, while tethered horses patiently swiped flies with their wiry tails.

Vera felt as though she'd fallen asleep reading *Hansel and Gretel* and awakened to find the evil witch stuffing her into the oven. Dream and fantasy had conquered reality.

A light tap on the door heralded Jericho's return.

His dark head peeked around the half-open door. "How was the grub?"

Despite herself, Vera rolled her eyes and smiled. "The best meal I've had in...in decades."

His dark brows dipped slightly, then he shrugged and smiled back. A rather nice smile, she thought. Too bad he didn't use it more often.

Closing the door behind him, he thrust his fists onto his narrow hips. "'Fraid I have some bad news.

There's been an accident at the mine—six miners are trapped.''

Vera frowned, sorry for the endangered workers but wondering what this could have to do with her.

As if reading her confusion, he continued, ''Doc Greavy'll be going from the Nesbitts' straight to the mine. He'll stay 'til they dig those fellas out, in case anybody's hurt.''

''So he won't be coming back to Jerome for a while,'' she concluded, as comprehension filled her. ''No problem, I'm feeling fine anyway.''

Jericho didn't reply but she knew from his dark scowl that he still believed she suffered from a head injury and needed medical attention.

Leaning his hip against a sturdy oak sideboard, he said, ''Every able-bodied man in town is headed out to the mine to help dig. Folks'll notice if I'm not there.''

Vera wondered if he meant his absence would raise suspicion as to her whereabouts or that his failure to help would hurt his business. Regardless of his motivation, she understood that he had to lend whatever help he could offer.

In fact, maybe she should go along. Vera had received training in disaster response, and, unfortunately, had far too much experience assisting in injury accidents. She could help the townspeople while perhaps picking up information about Rafe Wilson's murder.

Nodding abruptly, she said, ''We'd better get out to the mine then.''

Jericho's head reared back. "Whoa! You're not going anywhere, sugar. You'll be safe right here."

Vera felt her back stiffen. She wasn't his "sugar," nor was she about to take orders from this six-gun-toting Neanderthal. "I can help out there and I'm going."

"Is your brain completely addled? Those folks see you and they're apt to string up a rope right on the spot. No, you're not to set foot out of this room. You *sabe?*"

Memories of her rookie year surged forth. The first woman in her patrol unit, she'd been subjected to untold macho comments and unfair orders she'd been obliged to follow. But she'd served her probation, proven herself. She wasn't going to backtrack now.

Feeling a heated flush high on her cheeks, she leaned forward. "I really wish you hadn't said that. Get this straight, it's *my* life on the line—not yours. I'm not going to sit back like a good little girl and wait for a bunch of ignorant cowhands to slip a noose around my neck. *You sabe?*"

A long, tense pause ensued, then Jericho raised his hands, palms out, in resignation. "Don't go gettin' your knickers in a twist, sugar. You want to get your pretty little neck stretched, that's your business. Course you'd be the first woman hanged in these parts. First this year, anyway."

Vera's hand flew to her throat in an involuntary protective gesture. Perhaps Jericho had a point. It would be easier to clear herself if her toes weren't dangling from a sturdy tree limb.

Once, Vera had been "loaned" to the San Francisco PD for a sting operation. For three nights, she'd donned gaudy clothing and too much makeup, posing as a working girl plying her trade in one of the seedier areas of the vast city. After she'd gotten over the embarrassment of catcalls and whistles following her down the avenue, she'd found she actually enjoyed the covert operation and wished the CHP offered more opportunity for undercover work.

Looked like she was going to get her wish. If ever a situation called for subterfuge and stealth, this was it. Moving to the tall, gilt-edge mirror on the far wall, she stared at her image for a long moment. Finally, she turned to Jericho. "Earlier, you said you had girls working here. Think I could borrow some of their clothing?"

Jericho backed up, casting out those expressive hands like a sinner warding off a tempting offer from the devil. "Oh no you don't. Hanging's nothing compared to what your mother would do to me if I let you parade around town dressed like a saloon girl. No, siree. Absolutely not."

Obviously, he'd closed his mind to reason, and further argument would be to no avail. She had to remember that she was dealing with a man from the past, a man who didn't meet women on an equal plane. If her college history studies had been accurate, men of Jericho's time could only be persuaded through seduction and manipulation.

Even though using her feminine wiles wasn't in her usual arsenal of relationship tactics, she sensed it was the only method of persuasion that might be effective on the hardheaded Mr. Jackson.

Vera drew in a deep breath and called upon the meager acting skills she'd learned during the undercover sting operation. Forcing a slightly seductive smile onto her lips, she cocked her head to the side, and slowly crossed the room to stand in front of him.

Reaching up, she took the ends of his ribbon tie in her hands and straightened the bow, her fingertips lightly and deliberately brushing against the fine linen fabric of his shirt. "Now listen, Jericho, *sugar,* we need to talk about this."

He folded his arms across his chest and stood firm. "No ma'am, absolutely not. And that's my final word on the subject."

Chapter Five

Thirty minutes later, Vera demurely wrapped the hem of the bright red satin dress around her ankles and climbed onto the hard wooden bench seat of the buckboard wagon Jericho had rented from the livery stable. Since it was still early in the day, she'd abstained from donning the black-plumed hair decoration he'd fetched in favor of a heavy coating of pancake makeup and an ostentatious black beauty mark high on her cheekbone.

In Vera's opinion, she looked nothing like the faded photograph of Verity McBride, but did make a rather fetching dance hall floozie—if she could just ignore the rough texture of the mesh tights chafing her inner thighs. Still, she was confident that no one would mistake her for the outlaw girl.

"How far to the mine?" she asked.

"Not far enough. Your mama is gonna have my scalp if she gets wind of this. Heahh!" Jericho clicked his tongue and shook the reins, spurring the chestnut mare into action.

With a vicious jerk, the wagon bucked along the narrow rutted path up the mountain. If Vera had thought traversing the primitive trail was difficult on horseback, she'd sadly underestimated the degree of discomfort while bouncing up and down on a rough-planed wooden bench.

Twice she slipped her hand beneath her seat to yank out toothpick-size splinters that pierced her bottom. Certain that Jericho was encouraging the horse to move with more alacrity than he would normally employ, Vera glowered ferociously in his direction. If Jericho noted her discomfort, he gave no notice; instead, he continued to hum that tuneless tune he favored.

Giving up, she braced herself as best she could and thought about what they might find once they reached the mine entrance. She recalled her own brief hours trapped below the earth's surface and felt a strong empathy with the men who, if still alive, knew they might never again breathe fresh air into their oxygen-starved lungs.

She realized with a start that their pace had slowed considerably. The rickety wagon crawled around a hairpin curve as the tired horse negotiated the nearly vertical path. Despite herself, Vera leaned closer to Jericho, wanting to distance herself from the sheer drop-off plunging endlessly down the rock-strewn mountain to her right.

Keeping his attention tightly focused on the treacherous roadway, Jericho glanced briefly in her direction. "What's got you so spooked? You generally race up these curves like a wild goat."

She leaned further into him, the solid heft of his

upper arm offering tenuous comfort. "Just a little nervous today, I guess."

The path flattened slightly and Jericho leaned back, letting the trail-wise mare have her head once more. "Can't say as I blame you. If this disguise doesn't work, this might be your last morning as a free woman."

When she didn't reply, he continued, "You never said how you happened to bushwhack ole' Rafe in the first place."

Vera gasped. What was wrong with her? He'd mentioned before that Rafe Wilson had been ambushed, shot from behind. From reading Verity's journal, Vera knew that the younger woman had hit her stepfather with a cast iron frying pan. There'd been no mention of a shooting.

Slowly turning to Jericho, she spoke slowly, trying to quell her growing excitement. She didn't want him to think she was about to succumb to the vapors again. "There must be some mistake. Rafe wasn't shot. I, uh, he was hit with a skillet. In self-defense."

His black-eyed gaze drilled through her flimsy poise. "Hate to argue with you, sugar, but I saw the body myself. Rafe had a hole in his back nearly as big around as that bankroll he always carried in his hip pocket. I'd say he was picked off with a carbine from a safe distance."

Vera shook her head. "Don't you see? Someone framed Verity, um, me. Obviously, after the altercation in the cabin someone else came along and shot Rafe."

At long last the rocky trail evened out and Jericho

paused to give the hardworking steed a rest. Folding the leather reins across his lap, he assessed Vera. "Reckon you'd better tell your story now."

Eyes closed, she dredged up memory fragments from Verity's journal and related what she knew of the altercation between Rafe and Verity.

When she finished her recital, Jericho didn't respond immediately. For a long, thoughtful moment, he lowered his gaze, staring at his rock hard hands still holding the reins. He looked up, pinning her with his eyes and quietly asked, "When did this happen?"

Did he want a date? The day of the week? Without refreshing her memory with the journal, Vera couldn't recall such specific details. "It was almost dark when—"

"At night? You say you whacked Rafe at night?"

"Yes, that's right. It was cold, started snowing later."

"That would have been Tuesday night. Snow stopped around midnight. Your brother showed up looking for me Wednesday morning. Found you in the mine late that afternoon. But something's wrong with this yarn...when we rode out to the cabin we found Rafe's body in the snow. He hadn't laid there all night 'cause there wasn't any snow on top of him. He'd been shot that morning. Wasn't even stiff yet."

Excited, Vera grabbed his arm. "Don't you see? That proves Verity, er, I couldn't have done it! How could I have shot Rafe in the back, then raced to the Balbriggan mine fast enough to fall down a mine shaft before you arrived a couple hours later?"

Jericho's head tossed slowly from side to side.

"There was plenty of time to hotfoot it to the Balbriggan while your brother moseyed into town for help."

"But I didn't shoot him! Why can't you believe me?"

Jericho slowly tipped her chin upward and searched her pleading eyes. After a moment, he shook his head. "Reckon as how I do believe you, Ver, but I don't see how that's going to help much. Lots of folks 'round these parts didn't cotton much to Rafe Wilson, but, hell, nobody cared enough about him to shoot the sorry bastard."

Clinging to the touch of warmth in his dark gaze, she stated the obvious. "Somebody did."

DESPITE HIS UNDERLYING concern that someone might recognize the fugitive beneath her disguise, Jericho was nonetheless relieved when they rolled to a stop a hundred yards from the mine opening.

As sole owner of the Copper Penny saloon, Jericho had become accustomed to dealing with women and had developed an easy familiarity with the half-dozen women he employed. Hardly a week went by when he didn't have to referee some petty squabble, or wipe away tears from hurt feelings. While he made no claims to understanding the fair sex, he generally felt comfortable with women and could in time figure out what was going on under the surface.

Not so with Vera, as Verity now preferred to be called. She was as hard to figure out as a campaigning politician. And about as evasive. By turns she was vulnerable, strong, weepy, serene, smart as hell, addle-brained, and hot tempered as a Mexican chili pepper.

She kept him off-kilter and mad as a bee-stung viper most of the time. Yet she was more softly feminine, more downright alluring than any woman he'd ever known. Every time Vera came near enough to touch, Jericho felt a little jiggle in his heart and a tightening in his drawers. The woman was maddening.

Now, however, wasn't the time to dwell on Vera McBride, or her curious effect on him. He'd no sooner pulled the buckboard to the side of the trail when he was surrounded by a flurry of miners.

"Jackson, good to see you. Don't suppose you brought any samples from the bar?" Tug McMillan thumbed his broken suspender strap which he'd fastened to his trousers with a rusty safety pin.

"Not unless you count the fixins' for a pot of strong coffee," Jericho replied, holding aloft a huge blue graniteware coffeepot.

Jess Wiggins, a tall, powerfully built miner who always bullied his way to the center of attention, reminding Jericho of an aggressive bull elk, slid up to the wagon. "See you brought entertainment at least. Don't reckon I know this purty little thing."

Unaccountably irritated, Jericho snapped, "She's not here for your entertainment."

Wiggins reached into his pocket and held up a few coins. "Hey, Jackson, I don't expect something for nuthin'. I'm willing to pay for this purty gal's favors."

Catching a glimpse of Vera's repulsed face, Jericho

slapped aside the man's hands, ignoring the tinkle of silver coins falling to the ground. "You know I don't rent out my girls, Wiggins. They're paid to serve drinks and deal cards. No more."

Wiggins bent over to retrieve his money. "One of these days you're going to get too high-and-mighty for your own good, Jackson."

Ignoring the muttered threat, Jericho turned back to Tug McMillan. "So, what's happening here?"

Tug scratched his grizzled red beard. "Fire down in number three shaft at the four-hundred-foot level. Don't look good."

Jericho nodded. Dust from the sulphide ores was highly combustible, and, when dumped into a haulage shaft, often ignited spontaneously. Although bulkheads were erected to contain the frequent fires, they were often unsuccessful. Down at the United Verde Mine, they'd had a fire burning steadily in one of the shafts for several years. Jericho hoped they didn't have a similar situation here.

But he needn't have worried about anyone recognizing the fugitive he'd brought into their midst. Other than Jess Wiggins's lecherous interest, the other hundred or so people gathered around the mine opening had more serious matters concerning them than Jericho's new saloon girl.

Crossing to the other side of the wagon, he helped Vera to the ground. "Stay close to me and follow my lead," he whispered. With an arm slung casually around her shoulder, he led her to where a group of women were busily tearing sheeting material into bandages.

"Mornin', ladies." He tipped his black Stetson. "This here's my new chanteuse, Mizz Vera LaFleur. She thought maybe she could help care for the injured when we haul them out."

The oldest woman present, a short dumpling in a lavender calico dress sprigged with tiny yellow flowers, stepped forward and thrust out a pudgy hand. "Martha Femple, Mizz LaFleur. We'd be glad of the help."

Taking Vera's hand between her two smaller ones, Martha asked curiously, "What is it Jericho said you were?"

"A chanteuse," he repeated, not giving Vera a chance to object. "A singer. A world-famous entertainer we imported all the way from San Francisco, California to bring some culture to our town. I'm surprised you haven't heard of her."

Martha pressed a chubby finger against her cheek. "You know—I believe I have heard your name. A world-famous singer right here in Jerome. Oh, my."

The other women twittered in excitement.

Dropping her voice, Martha continued in a confidential tone, "You know, I used to sing in the choir before we left Saint Louis and some said my vocalizations were rather sweet." She raised her voice as if to ensure being overheard by her confederates. "I always thought I should have gone on the stage." She turned to treat the other women to a discourse on the difficulties of singing professionally.

"A singer!"

"How exciting!"

"Exciting is hardly the word," Vera murmured so

that Jericho alone would hear. She laid her hand on his shoulder and pressed her warm lips against his ear. "If these people ever have to *listen* to me sing, they'll probably string you up beside me."

Jericho ignored her stricken expression. She was just being modest. He'd once heard her singing a lullaby to one of the babies and thought she'd possessed a nice voice. At least she'd carried a tune. So when it came time to explain her presence to the townspeople, he'd decided "chanteuse" sounded more respectable than "saloon girl." Maybe Min-e-wah wouldn't be so quick to flay him alive.

Following Martha Femple's lead, the other women gathered close to introduce themselves, anxious to catch a firsthand glimpse of the glamorous "chanteuse."

Relieved by their ready acceptance, Jericho left Vera on her own to embellish the famous singer story and headed for the mine opening.

Before she had time to trip herself up in her own lies, a sharp cry from the mine entrance sent them all scurrying.

A man, his face coated with thick red dust, burst through the timbered mouth. "They're comin' out! We'll need ever' able-bodied man to help tote 'em."

The gathered men surged toward the mine in a single, eager swell. The women hurried to get a glimpse, too, each hoping in her heart that the men would be carried out alive.

Martha Femple was the first to dare voice her fear. "Are they all alive, Frankie?"

The dirt-shrouded miner shook his head. "Cain't

tell yet. Some are moanin' but others are dreadful still.''

He turned and darted back inside, followed by the sea of men ready to help their friends and co-workers.

The clearing was deserted, quiet. Then a young woman with a babe bundled in her arms started to sob. Martha moved swiftly but unobtrusively to her side and wrapped the younger woman in her ample arms. ''Don't fret, hon. Your man will be fine. You just wait and see.''

The seconds ticked by. Slowly. Dreadfully.

Then the muted sound of voices grew into a loud buzz and the women drew even closer to the opening. The first rescue team was coming out.

''Okay, ladies, you all step aside now and let me see to these fellas.'' A heavyset man of about forty lumbered off a wagon and pushed the gathered women aside. He swiped at a stream of perspiration that trickled down his face.

Carrying a homemade litter fashioned from a wool blanket and a couple of mop handles, four men dashed out of the mine with the first bloody miner.

They laid the inert body in front of the heavy man and stepped aside.

The large man, obviously the physician Jericho had referred to earlier, knelt over the injured miner. Before he could tell the assembled women whether or not his patient was still alive, the second rescue unit toted out another bloodied survivor. And another. And still another.

The small clearing broke into pandemonium.

The doctor hurried from one man to the next in an

obvious effort to triage the most desperately wounded. But he'd no sooner start to examine one, when someone would call him away.

Ignoring her pretty new dress, Vera stepped forward and tapped him on the shoulder. "I've had nursing experience. What can I do?"

"Roll up your sleeves." He rummaged in his bag and drew out several rolls of white bandage material. "Go around and try to stop all the bleeding if you can. If you find one that's hit a spurter, call me!"

Understanding that the man meant she should watch for anyone with a severed artery, Vera grabbed the bandages and ran to the nearest man.

She worked for thirty minutes, wiping, bandaging and running her practiced hand over arms and legs, searching for broken bones.

There were so many injured men scattered on the rocky red ground that it looked like a war zone. So far, thankfully, none of the men she'd treated had been fatally injured.

"Ma'am!" One of the rescue workers called out, "Over here!"

She patted the shoulder of the miner whose arm she'd just bandaged and raced across the clearing to examine the newest patient. His face was caked with heavy coppery dirt, segmented by streaks of bright red blood.

Grabbing a damp rag from the outstretched hand of one of the women, Vera swabbed his wound. He'd taken a blow to his left temple. Blood seeped out almost faster than she could blot it off.

Placing her fingertips slightly behind the seepage,

she applied enough pressure to slow the bloody flow. Keeping those fingers firmly in place, she swabbed around the wound with her other hand.

Although the gash was wide and long, it wasn't deep. She didn't know whether the doctor would be able to stitch it, but she did her best to fashion the bandage so it would hold the raw edges of the wound together.

When she'd finished, she took a clean cloth and wiped the man's face.

His eyes fluttered open and she saw he was young, not more than twenty-three or twenty-four. "Hi," she said softly. "Welcome back. How are you feeling?"

He licked his lips, leaving a clean streak on their parched surface. "Lucky to be alive, I reckon."

"Yorkie! How're you doing, boy?" Jess Wiggins leaned over her shoulder, his malodorous breath fouling the air.

"I'm doin' okay, I reckon. Least ways now that Miz Ver—"

Sensing what he was about to say, Vera hurriedly placed her fingertips on his lips. "Shhh. Don't talk."

She turned to Jess Wiggins. "He needs water. Would you ask one of the women to bring us some?"

He frowned, obviously displeased at being handed such a menial chore, but eventually grunted and stood up. "Anything for ole Yorkie."

When he'd moved away, she withdrew her fingers from the young man's lips. "Yorkie, is that your name?"

"Well, shucks, Miz Verity, you know that."

She glanced around to make sure he wasn't overheard. "No, I'm afraid you're mistaken. My name is Vera…LaFleur. I'm a singer at the Copper Penny."

Yorkie raised up on his elbows. "Well, I'll swan. Iffen you don't look to be the spittin' image of her." He shoved a large hand in her direction. "Folks call me Yorkie. Yorkie Delong. I'm from Louisiana, case you was wonderin'."

Smiling at the boy who seemed gifted with looks if not intelligence, she said, "Well, Yorkie, you seem to have survived the collapse without any serious damage. So, I'd better see if I can help someone else."

"That's okay, ma'am. You go on. But I surely do think you must be related to that girl of Rafe Wilson's."

"I don't think so," she murmured as she rose to her feet.

She smiled at the young man one last time and turned around.

Jess Wiggins was standing directly before her, a tin mug of water in his hand.

Vera swallowed. There was no way he'd missed Yorkie's last remark. No way.

She dipped her head in a slight nod and hurried around the burly miner. When she was ten feet away, she clasped her hands together to quell the trembling and slowly looked back.

Jess Wiggins was still standing in the same position, cup of water in his huge hand, staring at her.

Chapter Six

"I'm telling you I can't sing."

"Trust me, sugar, these ole boys aren't all that interested in your voice."

Vera stuck her head around the corner and grimaced. At least a hundred women-starved miners, farmers and assorted cowboys were gathered around the little stage in the corner. Two or three were already stamping their feet in anticipation. "Maybe I could just deal poker. I can *play* poker."

Jericho patted her bare shoulder and adjusted the black feather he'd stuck into her hair. "Nothing to it. Twitch your, er, seat a little and smile a lot, you'll have them lying at your feet."

She shuddered at the very image of a couple dozen filthy, *horny* miners groveling at her feet. *Think of this as an undercover assignment,* she repeated like a litany. The only way to approach these men was to make them trust her, make them want to answer her questions. She could do this. She could. Vera tossed her head, elevating her chin. "All right, don't say I didn't warn you. But I'm not twitching anything!"

Thunderous applause followed her slow passage to

the tiny stage. Nodding once to the piano accompanist, Vera broke into the modest repertoire they'd rehearsed earlier in the day. Realizing that she would never be confused with a balladeer, Vera had hummed the only three songs whose words she knew. Not surprisingly, Hank the pianist had never heard any of them. Still, after four hours' work they'd smoothed out a couple tunes she hoped she could carry.

Now, smiling at her eager audience, she waited for her musical cue and sang the opening line to "Proud Mary."

The miners loved the raucous beat. By the end of the number, toes were tapping and the men were singing the chorus of "rolling on the river" better than Vera. Feeling a bit more confident, she surged without a break into "American Pie" and ended up with a rousing rendition of a medley of show tunes.

Despite her initial misgivings, Vera LaFleur was an instant success.

When she stepped down from the stage, with the gentle assistance of at least a dozen men, she heard a familiar voice over the din. "Mizz LaFleur, over here."

Looking up, Vera spotted the burly Jess Wiggins beckoning her. "I've got us a table," he called.

Jess Wiggins was the last person in Jerome she wanted to share a drink with, but Jericho had told her earlier that Wiggins was one of Rafe's buddies. No one was more likely to have information about Rafe's business dealings. If she wanted to solve this murder so she could concentrate on getting back to her own time, she had to push aside her personal repugnance and pretend to enjoy Wiggins' company.

Smiling brightly, Vera crossed the room and took the chair he was holding out for her. He frankly eyed her cleavage. "Jackson wasn't storyin'. You sing sweeter 'n a morning warbler. What can I fetch you?" He broke off as another man approached the table. "Get the hell outta here, Yorkie. Can't you see the lady's with me?"

The young man called Yorkie smiled shyly. "But I just wanted to thank Miz LaFleur for patching me up today."

"Hello, Yorkie, I'm glad to see you're feeling better."

He patted the bandage that circled his head. "Yes ma'am, I do feel some better."

"Good," Wiggins said tersely. "Now, go find somebody to buy you a drink."

Yorkie shuffled his hat in his hands as if he wanted to say more, but when Wiggins started to stand up, the younger man waved and swiftly moved away.

"Damned cheats, always trying to jump somebody else's claim. Don't know what Rafe saw in that useless kid. What was it you said you wanted?"

"Beer," she answered, her voice a faint reed. Obligingly, he whistled for one of the bar girls. "Hey, Sweet Sue, bring us two beers and two shots."

Why, Vera wondered, hadn't she taken Drama 101 in high school? Pretending to enjoy Wiggins' company was going to stretch her acting ability beyond its limits.

While they waited for their drinks to arrive, she

pondered how to approach the subject of Rafe Wilson. "You work at the mine?"

"Don't ever'body?" he snorted.

The waitress approached. She leaned against the table, her hand pressed on her outthrust hip. With a toss of her suspiciously flame-colored hair, she smacked Wiggins on the shoulder. "Pay up. I ain't got all night, you know."

"Susannah, all you got is time." Jess slapped her backside through her ruffled green dress and dropped two coins on her tray. After giving Vera a frankly curious once-over, she shrugged and walked off.

Wiggins handed a foaming, warm tankard of beer to Vera, and clinked her mug with his. "Here's to a long, and *close* friendship."

Vera smiled tightly. "To friendship," she agreed. After she'd swiped the foamy residue from her upper lip, she tried again to broach the subject of Rafe Wilson. "I heard one of the foremen was killed the other day."

Wiggins frowned and shook his head. "You was at the mine when we hauled the boys out yestiddy. They all made it."

"No. I was talking about a few days ago. Wasn't one of the foremen killed?"

He thunked his mug onto the scarred table, golden liquid sloshing over the edge. "You must mean Rafe. Yeah, that murderin' bitch shot him."

Leaning closer, Vera chose her words carefully. "I thought there was some…uncertainty, as to who actually killed him."

"Uncertainty! Where you from? Talk like a over-schooled city woman. There weren't no uncertainty about it. That snooty half-breed stepdaughter of his did it.''

His rage shimmered like a fetid odor between them. Vera edged away. She wanted to drop the subject, wanted to get away from this disagreeable man altogether, but too much depended on him. If she wanted to stay alive long enough to escape this nightmare that had shoved her out of her own world, she had to clear Verity's name. And Jess Wiggins was the only lead she had.

To allow time for his temper to subside, she asked, ''What did you think of the show?''

A grin split his face, exposing tobacco-browned teeth. Two were missing altogether. ''Now that was somethin'. Never heard such songs. Can't say as I understood what you was getting at, but had a good time listening. Say, what *is* a Chevy, anyhow?''

Vera knew he was referring to a line in one of the songs where she sang about driving a Chevy to the levee. For one tantalizing moment, she was tempted to tell Jess Wiggins that it was a popular make automobile, and that the song was in fact a tribute to a rock singer from the early '50s. The 1950s.

She sighed. It would be fun to watch his reaction, but with her recent luck, she'd surely end up in a loony bin. ''It's a brand of buggy. Haven't you heard of them? They're all the rage in San Francisco.''

Wiggins nodded slowly, greasy, unkempt hair flopping over his eyes. ''Yeah, reckon I have at that. So, tell me, purty lady, what brings you out here?''

Anxious to get the conversation back on track,

Vera replied, "I've always been fascinated with stories about Arizona. Gunfighters, mines, things like that. Guess that's why I'm so interested in that man who was shot the other day. What was his name? Ray Wilson?"

"Rafe. Rafe Wilson. Don't know why you'd take on so about that. Weren't much of a puzzle. His squaw's kid plugged him. Ungrateful whelp. After Rafe took her in and fed her all these years, she just up and shot him."

"But I heard a different story. I heard there'd been a fight and that the girl hit him with a pan or something."

"Then you heard wrong. Why are you taking up for a cold-blooded murderer?"

"I didn't realize she'd been convicted."

"She ain't been caught yet. Then she'll be convicted. And hanged."

"You don't seem to have any doubt about her guilt."

"Who else woulda hurt Rafe? He was ornery on occasion, but not bad oncet you got to know him."

Vera pretended to ponder his question. "Maybe someone he owed money to, a gambling debt, perhaps? Or a business associate. Did Rafe have any business interests outside the mine?"

Scratching his grizzled beard with his fingernails, Wiggins seemed to consider her question. "He was an enterprising sort. Had a lot of irons in the fire. Matter of fact, he was goin' on the other day about some discovery he'd made. Said he'd got himself a business pardner."

"There you go then," Vera replied with a smile. "Doesn't it make more sense that he would have been killed over a business deal rather than by his stepdaughter? Do you know who that partner is?"

"Nope. No reason to care, neither. Verity McBride murdered her pa."

Vera sighed. How could she make this man question his unfounded certainty? Why were these people so set on convicting Verity of the murder? Hoping that her tone was reasonable and not filled with the frustration she felt, Vera asked, "What was Verity's motive? You said Rafe supported her...why would she kill her only source of support?"

Wiggins drained the contents of the two shot glasses of potent-smelling whiskey and stared at Vera. "How come you're so interested in this? You act like you've got a personal stake in Rafe's murder."

"I just don't want that girl to be hanged for something she might not have done."

He leaned closer until his vile breath wreathed her face. His voice dropped to a near whisper. "I don't suppose you know where that girl's hiding, do you? Seems to me you're askin' a passel of questions about something that ain't no concern of yourn. How come?"

The air shimmered with the heated undercurrent of his observation. The background laughter and tinkle of glasses faded into oblivion as time seemed to pause—awaiting her reply.

Vera sat back and held her breath until the stench of his breath faded. "No, no particular reason. Just making conversation."

Wiggins stood up and kicked his chair aside. Bending low, until his filthy face was only inches from hers, he intoned, "You know, it ain't hardly wise for a stranger to come around askin' questions about things what don't concern her."

Vera felt the hairs on the back of her neck rise in response to his thinly veiled threat. She wasn't used to intimidation tactics. When she encountered men of his ilk during her duties as a highway patrol officer, they were far more conciliatory in hopes of escaping a traffic citation. Wiggins's threatening manner made her want to reach for her wrist restraints, which, unfortunately, hadn't yet been invented in 1896. Besides, her better judgment warned that she'd gain more information by adhering to her undercover persona.

"There's no need to get upset," she forced a purr into her voice. "I told you I was just talking."

"Oh, you ain't seen me riled yet," Wiggins snapped, apparently not in the least placated by her response. "I'm just warning you that a purty face ain't liable to hold back the hangman. You seem to be taking a little too much interest. I'd watch my step if I was you. Evenin' ma'am."

He straightened, glancing around the bar as if making sure their conversation hadn't been overheard. With a slight tip of his stained hat, Jess Wiggins strode out of the bar.

Vera watched him leave, still taken aback by the virulence of his reaction to her questions. Why had he been so prickly? If Wiggins's only role in the death of Rafe Wilson was that of bereaved friend, why was he so unwilling to talk about it? Wiggins seemed determined that Verity McBride, and no other, should be blamed for the shooting.

She was still pondering when she sensed a presence approaching. Glancing over her shoulder, Vera encountered Jericho's dark eyes warily watching her.

Using his booted foot, he drew out the chair Wiggins had just vacated and straddled it, folding his long arms across the curved wooden back. "Never seen Jess Wiggins go home so early on a Friday night. You two didn't hit it off?"

Vera rolled her eyes. "No, I'm afraid not. And I'm so brokenhearted."

"You didn't have to sit with him. That's not part of your job."

What was that harsh edge she detected in his tone? Irritation? Jealousy? She tossed her head, dislodging the ridiculous thought. Jericho Jackson had no interest in her. And given their...peculiar circumstances, she might as well ignore that odd pitty-pat in her stomach whenever he came close. Not much point in fostering a relationship when their lives were separated by more than a century. This was an entanglement she'd like to see Dear Abby resolve.

Forcing her thoughts back on his comment, she nodded slowly. "Speaking of job descriptions—"

"Pardon?"

"Sorry. That's a term from my ti— I mean, a term they use in California."

Jericho stared into her eyes for a long, piercing moment. "How is it you know so much about California? You've never been out of Arizona."

Vera exhaled a deep breath, ruing yet another slip of the tongue. Every conversation was fraught with danger. Jericho obviously thought she was mentally unhinged. If she told him the truth, he would have no doubts. She had to be more careful, keep everything she said conversational, inane. "Guess I've read a lot. Newspapers."

"Uh-huh."

She sensed he was going to question her again so she leaned forward and changed the subject, hoping to break off further inquiry. "You said it wasn't part of my job to sit with the customers. What about the other women who work here—do they have to sit with the men?"

When he didn't answer right away she found herself wondering why his means of employment was so important to her. True, no one wanted a friend who was involved in unsavory activities. She was uneasily aware that her growing feelings for this enigmatic man were quickly surpassing mere friendship. As she waited in breathless anticipation for his response, she found herself half hoping he'd admit to the allegation and thereby nip her developing interest to the bud.

Shifting his hooded gaze, Jericho glanced around the crowded barroom, looking over one shoulder then the other. "Yep. That's what I pay them for—to entertain the customers. There aren't a lot of available women in these parts. The men like having someone soft and feminine to spill their troubles to."

Running her fingertip around the rim of her empty beer glass, she asked nonchalantly, "And that's all they have to do? Talk?"

"What exactly are you asking?"

Vera shrugged. "I just wanted to know what those rooms upstairs are used for."

"Sleeping." Jericho pushed away from the table and strode back to the bar.

Susannah, the waitress who'd brought their drinks sauntered over. "Looks like you're not having a real good night, honey."

Vera looked up at the woman's guileless face, but couldn't ignore the burning stares of the miners at the nearby tables. Ducking her gaze from their unbridled curiosity, she asked, "Was my voice that bad?"

Susannah tucked a strand of bloodred hair behind her ear and picked up Wiggins's empty glasses. "Wasn't talking about your singing. The men liked you just fine."

"What, then?"

Cocking her head at Jericho's stiff back leaning against the bar, Susannah leaned forward, not bothering to hide her avid curiosity. "You ran off two of the town's most eligible bachelors in ten minutes flat. I'd say that was the town record."

Vera laughed wryly. "I'd hate to think things were so bad in this town that Jess Wiggins is considered a catch."

"He takes a bit of getting used to, I'll grant you that." The redhead picked up the tray of glasses and turned toward the bar. She paused and looked back at Vera. "All the same, it's a might strange, seeing how the most hound-ugly woman usually can't discourage Jess Wiggins."

Vera drained her beer mug and stood up; it was time for her second show. "Sue, this has been a strange week any way you look at it. Trust me on that."

Chapter Seven

Jericho watched through the wide, smoky mirror behind the bar as yet another facet of Vera's complex personality unfolded. The shy gangly girl he'd known as Verity was submerged beneath the stronger, more sexually potent personality of the woman who called herself Vera. Now, in the somewhat bawdy third incarnation of Vera LaFleur, another surface was revealed.

He'd given up trying to make sense of what had happened to Verity—or of the words of the songs she warbled in a slightly off pitch but huskily pleasant voice. Instead, he preferred to watch that unconscious grinding of her womanly hips, the coy yet frankly sensual glances she cast at the hooting cowpokes who made up her appreciative audience.

If it wasn't for the vengeful posse hell-bent on stringing her up, Jericho would be tempted to take Vera LaFleur up on that tantalizing promise her pouting lips revealed. Tempted, hell. If her very life wasn't on the line, he'd have her in his bed tonight.

A gentle shudder teased his loins at the thought of Vera's warm body squirming beneath his touch, her thick sheaf of dark hair only partially veiling her nudity.

The song ended and Vera lightly descended from the small stage. Catcalls and boots stomping on the wooden floor hailed her progress across the saloon. As she came up behind him, Jericho quickly glanced down into his tankard of beer. He was still stung from her insinuation that he was running a bawdy house. Of all people, she should know better.

His back tingled as Vera stopped behind him. Just as he was about to turn and grin, and save her the embarrassment of having to offer an apology, she turned and stalked toward the stairs. Jericho downed the dregs of his tankard. The hell with her. Jericho elbowed his way through the rowdy crowd and stomped outside.

The night had cooled sharply but the clear sky, polka-dotted with sparkling starlight was a welcome sign. Not likely to snow. Snow kept the miners and cowboys alike penned up; snow in the mountains was bad for business. Snow would also slow down the men who were combing the scrubby hills for Verity McBride.

Jericho felt like the condemned man who didn't know whether to pray for a rope or a bullet. A healthy snowfall would be good news for Verity but disastrous for him.

Turning on his heel, he strode down the sidewalk, the rowels on his spurs jangling with each step. Except for the raucous voices and muted music seeping out of the dozen saloons that dotted the main thoroughfare, the night was eerily quiet.

"Psst! Mr. Jackson."

He turned his head toward the whispered voice and caught a slight flicker of movement in the dark alley. "Who's there? Come out so I can see you."

A hesitant rustling noise, then a form emerged from the shadows. Verity stood in the moonlight, a heavy drover's coat sagging to the ground around her feet. Her ink dark hair was hidden beneath a stained and rumpled bowler hat. Only her face was recognizable.

Jericho stepped toward her. "What are you doing out here? I told you not to leave the hotel without me."

Her dark eyebrows fluttered in surprise. "Mr. Jackson, I haven't *been* to the hotel. Didn't my brother get word to you? I've been holding out at that old line shack at the Balbriggan."

His heart thudded in his chest. She'd gone off again. Her mind, obviously weakened from the stressful events, had wandered into that strange place he couldn't fathom. "Verity—I mean, Vera, why don't you come on back to the hotel with me?"

She tossed her head. "No. I just need to ask if I can borrow your horse, maybe a bite of food for the road. I have to go to my mother's people. I'll be safe there."

Forcing himself to remain calm, he inched closer and placed his hands on her frail shoulders. "That's what I've been trying to tell you, that you need to get out of town. Soon as Doc Greavy gets back, we'll get you to the Apache encampment. I promise."

Her head jerked up. "Why would I want to see

Doc Greavy? That old buzzard'll turn me in quick as spit.''

"No," Jericho gripped her shoulders tightly, feeling like the last line of defense between this defenseless girl and the men who would imprison her. A few moments ago, Vera was a strong, enticing woman. But that woman had evaporated into this still softly vulnerable girl. With her personas, she seemed to actually physically change. He was suddenly ashamed of those carnal thoughts that had been entertaining him most of the evening. "You have to let me help you."

She pulled from his grasp. "I know my way and I don't need no doctor. Just give me some food and the use of your horse and I'll hightail it out of here and you'll be shed of me and my troubles."

Realizing he couldn't reach her in this present incarnation, Jericho nodded slowly. If he could lure her back to the hotel, maybe he could stall her departure long enough for Doc Greavy's return. "I'll go over to the livery stable and get one of my horses saddled up. You head on over to the hotel. Go in the back door. No one's in the kitchen now. Wait there for me. Shouldn't take long."

"Thank you, Mr. Jackson," she breathed. "I appreciate all you've done for me and my kin."

"There isn't enough I can do to repay my debt to your mother. Go on, now, before someone sees you. I'll be along shortly."

Without another sound, the slender girl in the heavy coat melted into the night.

VERA PACED across the dark hotel room, stopping every few seconds to glance out the window. Jericho had marched down the street nearly an hour ago and hadn't returned. Where had he gone?

He'd been clearly miffed with her downstairs. Did he now regret helping her? Maybe he'd gone to find the deputy sheriff and turn her in. Vera didn't want to think about that other possibility. The one that whispered he was seeking solace from her bruising words in the arms of one of the "fancy" women at Rosie's Sporting House.

Unable to stand the silent accusations of the lonely room any longer, she donned her jeans and sweatshirt and slipped out of the room. A glass of warm milk might soothe her frayed nerves. She had to think. Figure out this unfathomable mess she'd literally fallen into.

Taking the back staircase so no one would spot her in her peculiar attire, Vera stole downstairs to the kitchen. Her hand was on the swinging wood-paneled door when she heard the hum of muted voices. Someone was in the room.

Her heart ka-whumped to a double-time beat. Had Jericho betrayed her after all? Was he even now outlining a plan with the posse to take her into custody? No, please God, she prayed, anything but that.

She pressed her ear flat against the door but could only pick up the indecipherable murmur of two voices speaking in a conspiratorial whisper. Taking a deep breath, she eased the door open enough to allow a peek.

Jericho's back was to her. His booted foot was

propped on the lower rung of a battered kitchen chair, his elbow propped on his knee as he spoke in an earnest tone to the person seated before him. Vera couldn't see who was in the chair. She could only tell from the soft voice that it was a woman. And Jericho was speaking softly and tenderly.

Vera couldn't understand the sting of hurt and rejection that lashed her insides. Jericho Jackson was a real man with a real life before she'd dropped into his world. Why was she surprised to discover he had a special woman in his life? And why did the realization throb like a cankered tooth?

Easing the door closed, she backed down the hallway until her heel struck the bottom stair and she tumbled backward in an unceremonious heap.

The voices stilled suddenly and Vera heard the heavy tread of Jericho's boots crossing the hotel kitchen. She couldn't let him see her! The only thing worse than the knowledge of his loving another woman would be for him to witness her humiliation at having been caught eavesdropping.

Leaping to her feet, Vera scrambled up the steps just as the door to the kitchen opened wide.

"Hello? Anybody there?"

Pausing on the landing, Vera pressed her back into the wall until it seemed she would surely burst through the plaster.

"Is someone out here?"

The slow creak of wooden floorboards beneath his feet foreshadowed his approach. Hand over her mouth, Vera eased farther into the shadows. The footsteps stopped, paused, then receded as Jericho went back into the kitchen.

She exhaled in a long, relieved breath and hurried back to Jericho's apartment. Inside, she ran for the bedroom and slid beneath the covers, fully clothed. Lying in the dark she thought back over the events of the past two days. Had the world gone mad or had her own mind taken flight from reality?

She'd already given up on the hope that she was living through an extended dream; no, somehow, she'd flown through a time warp and landed in a time period whose people and customs she couldn't accept or understand.

What had she been thinking—that she was attracted to this poor man's version of Rhett Butler? That she could find a way to take him with her back to her future? Or had she imagined she would just stay here in the past and live among the illiterate miners, over-worked housewives and sad prostitutes that populated this mining town?

Get real, she snorted in self-disgust. *Like you'd be happy hauling water and darning socks for a chauvinist piglet like Jericho Jackson.*

Vera was a realist, a woman who knew who she was and where she was headed in life. She loved her job and sought greater responsibility, knowing full well that the price of her dedication might mean that she'd spend her life alone. Few men of her world were emotionally equipped to marry a female cop, a woman who didn't need their protection or financial support. And she'd entertained the notion that Jericho might be evolved enough to welcome a strong, self-reliant woman into his life?

The very idea was laughable.

No, it was a blessing she'd stumbled upon Jericho and his female companion. Vera had been too taken by his overt sexual appeal to think clearly. She should be glad for the slap of reality. Now she could forget all about Mr. Jackson's sexy butt and concentrate on getting back to her own time.

The answer, she was suddenly certain, would be found somewhere in Verity McBride's journal. Vera turned up the wick on the oil lamp and pulled the journal from the drawer. Leaning back against the pillows, she pushed Jericho from her mind and tried to concentrate on the words her ancestor had penned.

What Vera couldn't easily ignore was the raw ache centered somewhere around her heart.

THE NEXT MORNING Jericho stood in the open doorway to his bedroom and stared in surprise at the lovely apparition snuggled in his bed.

What was she doing here? Last night he'd saddled a horse, loaded her saddlebags with food and water and pressed money into her hand. Then he'd served as lookout until she'd safely escaped the town proper, disappearing in the darkness on her way down to Verde Valley. Jericho had never expected to see her again, yet, unbelievably, here she was curled in his bed as if she belonged there!

Looking at her face, soft and trusting in sleep, he felt another stab of wishful thinking. Why hadn't he seen the promise of such powerful womanhood in Verity before Rafe's murder?

And what had gone so terribly wrong with her that she kept slipping in and out of herself, forgetting simple things she'd known her entire life? Well, before her mental confusion cost Verity her life, he had to do what he could to help.

Nodding decisively, Jericho slipped out of the room and headed back downstairs to the hotel dining room where Doc Greavy had been shoveling in a healthy pile of flapjacks a few moments ago.

The corpulent physician had finished his breakfast and was sitting back, savoring a mug of coffee, his sausagelike fingers tapping against the rim of the steaming brew. He was holding court like a despotic ruler. His audience, unfortunately, included Jess Wiggins.

Jericho slid into the vacant chair between Wiggins and Yorkie Delong, directly across from Stuart Greavy. "Mornin', Doc. Fellas."

Cursory greetings were exchanged before they returned to the ongoing discussion.

Wiggins fingered his stubbled chin. "Doc here says the posse's on their way in."

That wasn't good news. Since their thoughts had been locked on finding Verity for the past few days, someone might see through her Vera LaFleur disguise. Pretending only mild interest, Jericho said, "That right? Then she's on the way to the Prescott jail or are they bringing her back here?"

"Nope, she done got clean away," Yorkie offered.

Jericho's eyebrows rose. "How's that possible?

There were what...almost a dozen men looking for that girl?"

Doc Greavy shrugged. "Nonetheless, she appears to have outwitted the lot of them."

"It's in her blood," Wiggins said blackly. "Rafe never should've taken that squaw in. Apaches have always been cutthroats, always will be."

Jericho had heard that familiar refrain enough to know where Wiggins was headed. *The only good Indian was a dead Indian*—in the eyes of far too many of his acquaintances. Anxious to deflect the discussion from Verity, he leaned forward. "Get that new youngun of Mrs. Nesbitt's into the world?"

Doc sipped his coffee and shook his head. "The little beggar didn't wait for me. Another hardheaded boy."

Wiggins snorted. "What's that make for ole' Luther, five...six boys now? He sure fires a loaded pistol."

Fearing the conversation was going to degenerate into a long discussion of Luther Nesbitt's sexual prowess, Jericho broke in. "Say, Doc, if you've got a few minutes I'd like to see you up in my room."

"Sure, what's the problem?"

Jericho's glance shifted to Wiggins and Yorkie. "Kind of, er, private, Doc, if you know what I mean."

The heavy man drained his coffee and pushed back from the table. "Why, Jericho, you're not embarrassed by a...social ailment passed on by one of Miz Rosie's ladies, now are you?"

Jericho allowed a sheepish grin to cross his face.

"Now don't go spreading a rumor like that, Doc. Might hurt my snow-white reputation."

His companions roared at the joke and Jericho led the way upstairs to his apartment. Doc Greavy's breath was heaving in his chest by the time they climbed the last few steps. Jericho opened the door and ushered the panting man inside.

"Sit down a minute and take a load off." Jericho nodded toward the horse hair sofa.

The doctor was only too happy to comply and sank into the cushions. He fished out a handkerchief, stained to a dull red by multiple washings in the mineral rich local water, and mopped his face. Leaning back, he asked, "So what's the problem, son? You aren't stupid enough to crawl into the sack with a diseased woman."

Jericho pulled over a side chair and faced the doctor. He had to word his request very carefully. Greavy was a respected leader in Jerome; he might balk at helping a suspected felon. Jericho decided to ease into the problem. "You really figure that girl killed Rafe Wilson?"

Greavy's wiry eyebrows raised in surprise. "You have evidence to the contrary?"

"No. Only that I've known her since she was knee-high to a bullfrog and killing a man in cold blood just isn't in her."

"You know better than that, son. Pushed against the wall, even the most peaceable folks will defend themselves."

Jericho shook his head. "This isn't about defending. This is about back-shooting, and Verity Mc-Bride's no back shooter.''

"Maybe not. But why doesn't she turn herself in and tell her story to a jury? That's what an innocent person would do.''

"Maybe she doesn't even realize what's going on.''

"Then where is she? Why'd she and her whole family hightail it outta town?'' Greavy shoved the damp hanky into his coat pocket.

"Seems to me we're jumping to a whole lot of conclusions, Doc. If Verity was a white woman, we'd've asked questions first. Not sent a posse out to hunt her down like a mad dog.''

"You've got a point, son, but you can't change the ignorant ways of a whole territory.''

Jericho's fist slammed on his knee. "Ignorance is no excuse!''

Greavy didn't reply for a long moment as he quietly assessed the younger man. "So, what is it you're asking me to do?''

"I'm asking you to remember you're a doctor first. Didn't you take some kind of vow to help everybody?''

"The Hippocratic oath, that's right. Are you trying to tell me that you know where that girl is? That she's injured?''

Jericho nodded wordlessly.

Greavy closed his eyes and appeared to think about Jericho's request. Finally he looked up. "That code I mentioned also guarantees a patient a degree of confidentiality. Reckon I can stretch that to mean I shouldn't disclose her whereabouts. At least until her wounds are healed up.''

"That's all I'm askin', Doc.''

"Then I give you my word,'' the doctor gravely intoned. "Now where is the young lady and what's her injury?''

Dropping his voice, Jericho filled the doctor in on Verity's oddly fluctuating behavior for the past two days. "It's almost like she's two entirely different people,'' he finished. "Until her mental confusion's cured, it's impossible for her to get a fair trial. She might say anything, admit to anything. Even if she didn't do it. If we turn her in now, we might as well just string her up ourselves.''

"I see your point. Mental confusion, loss of memory. I've read of similar cases in my medical journals. Difficult to treat, I'm afraid.''

"You gotta try, Doc.''

Greavy heaved his bulk off the sofa. "All right. Let's see what we can do.''

An hour later, he snapped the latch of his black satchel and stood up. He turned to Jericho. "Perhaps I can speak with you outside?''

"Oh, no you don't!'' Vera reached out and grabbed the heavy man's wrist. For the past hour she'd endured his questions, probing and other indignities. No way was she going to be dismissed like a naughty child while the "adults'' discussed her condition in the other room. "I want to hear every word.''

Greavy turned to Jericho and cocked a questioning eyebrow. When Jericho nodded, he said, "All right. As you wish. It's my opinion, young lady, that you are in excellent physical condition—exceptional actually. I don't believe I've ever examined a woman whose musculature is as well developed as yours.''

Vera decided not to mention the three hours a day she spent at the gym using free weights and boxing with a male sparring partner. ''I try to keep fit.''

''Uh-huh. Well, as I said your, uh, physique is in excellent condition. But your mind is another matter entirely. I don't know if you can truly appreciate what I'm saying, Miz McBride, but your brain seems to have suffered an injury. You have a large contusion just behind the left ear which probably accounts for your muddleheadedness.''

Muddleheadedness! Vera was about to expound on the good doctor's own lack of mental acuity when Jericho, as if reading her mind, stepped between them.

''So, what's the cure? Do you have some powders or tonics to help her?''

''I'm afraid not. The only thing I can prescribe is total bed rest. No excitement. Sometimes memory and clear thinking return in a few days. Sometimes, unfortunately, the patient remains in this state of bewilderment. Time, I'm afraid, is the only hope.''

He picked up his bag and started for the bedroom door. ''I'll check in again in the morning. But I warn you, undue excitement can be detrimental to your health, young lady.''

''Thank you, doctor,'' she smiled weakly. If that pompous ass called her ''young lady'' in that patronizing tone one more time, Vera wouldn't be responsible for her reaction. She contented herself by imagining how surprised he'd be if she gave him a stiff-fingered jab to the solar plexus.

Chapter Eight

"The poor girl is terribly addled." Doc Greavy shook his head, his tone a funereal murmur.

Jericho took the physician's arm and led him away from the closed door. They stood just outside his room. He didn't want Vera's tender spirit further bruised by overhearing the doctor's blunt words. "Is there nothing we can do for her?"

Greavy rubbed his chin and stared thoughtfully into the air. "Not much, I'm afraid. Complete rest is the only possible hope. Perhaps in a few weeks her...soul will return."

Jericho was hesitant to accept this advice. For one thing, he didn't think Vera's "soul" was lost, just a few of her memories seemed to be misplaced. Secondly, he was wary of keeping her confined to his apartment—her continued presence would surely cause talk.

Eventually, someone would connect the sudden appearance of the mysterious chanteuse with the sudden *disappearance* of Verity McBride. Heavy makeup, different hairstyle and clothing could only confuse the issue for so long.

"Course," Greavy continued, "her craziness might be a good defense. If she can convince a jury that she's tetched in the head, they might agree to let her live out the rest of her days in a sanitarium someplace."

Jericho suppressed a shudder. He'd heard about the appalling conditions in those "hospitals" for the insane. He couldn't condemn her to spend her life in such a dreadful place. No. There had to be another way.

"How is she otherwise?" he asked. "Physically, I mean."

"Oh, fit as a fiddle, I'd say," Greavy chortled. "A mite more, er, filled out than I recalled."

Jericho's head jerked up. So the doctor had noticed it, too! Last night, when Verity had appeared in the alley, and later in the kitchen, despite the bulky overcoat she'd worn, he'd had the impression of a scrawny, frightened young girl.

But when he'd returned to his apartment and found "Vera," the shift in her appearance had been incredible. Her figure was more...lush, full in all the right places. Her voice was lower-pitched, sensual. A woman in every sense of the word.

But a woman who was in danger.

For the first time in his life, Jericho felt completely helpless. The futility of his efforts infuriated him. Slamming his fist against the door frame, he stared into Greavy's eyes. "Are you telling me there's absolutely nothing I can do to help her?"

After a brief pause, the doctor nodded. "Maybe. I'll send around a bottle of medicine this afternoon.

Put four or five drops in a glass of water and give it to her before bed and every twelve hours afterward. It'll help her sleep. Plenty of sleep just might relax her enough so's her mind can mend itself.''

Grateful to be able to help in some small way, Jericho readily agreed to administer the dosage.

''Now in her state she might not want to take the medicine,'' Greavy warned.

''She'll take it. I'll make certain.''

''I'll have Yorkie bring it around shortly,'' the doctor said. ''Give her the first dose around ten tonight. Don't forget.''

''I won't.''

After thanking the doctor and stuffing some cash into his hand, Jericho stepped back inside the apartment. Tapping lightly on the bedroom door, he entered at Vera's command.

Wearing one of Jericho's shirts as a nightdress, she sat up against a mountain of pillows, a battered book open on her lap. When he entered the room she closed the book and laid it on the bedside table.

''So, what's the diagnosis? Am I certifiable and condemned to a home for the criminally insane?''

Cringing at how closely she'd targeted Greavy's diagnosis, he cast about for a shift of subject. He pointed to the book on the bedside. ''What're you reading?''

Vera tapped the worn cover. ''A journal.''

''Yours?''

She smiled, a strange enigmatic smile that made a gentle mockery of his question. ''In a manner of speaking, yes. You never told me what the good doctor had to say.''

Seeing she wasn't going to be distracted, he lowered onto the edge of the bed. ''He said the only thing that might help ease your…confusion…is for you to stay in bed for a while. And he's sending some medication.''

''Stay in bed! Mental illness, if that's what he thinks I'm suffering from, can't be helped by bed rest. Besides, I need to be downstairs, meeting the people, searching for information that might help me find Rafe Wilson's real murderer. I can't waste my time lolling about in bed.''

She started to rise but Jericho's firm hand pressed her back against the mound of pillows. ''You're going to stay right where you are.''

''But it's a waste of time!''

''So what are you now? A doctor, too? What makes you think you know better than him?''

''About a hundred years of more knowledge than he has,'' she snapped.

Jericho waggled his hand in the air. ''Whoa, aren't we the high-and-mighty one so pleased with ourself?'' He flicked his hand toward the book on the bedside table. ''So, you figure you've read a hundred years' more information than an educated man like Doc Greavy?''

''Exactly. If he's such an accomplished physician, why's he wasting his time in a jerkwater town like Jerome?''

The moment the words escaped her lips, Vera wished with all her heart she could have them back.

The slash of pain that darkened Jericho's features stabbed her with the force of a Bowie knife.

He stood up slowly. She couldn't gauge the emotion that glittered in his dark eyes but she could hear the barely contained quiver of rage in his voice. "Yeah, we ignorant clods who live in this jerkwater town are surely beneath your exalted stature. But right now, we're the only people standing between you and an early grave. So you'll stay in this room and you'll follow every bit of advice the doctor prescribes, or you'll find yourself out on the street again. See how long it takes these jerkwater natives to find a rope to fit your superior neck!" He turned and stalked from the room, the door reverberating in his wake.

Vera flopped back against the pillows. That was clever, she berated herself. She'd allowed her own frustration to mutate into displaced anger—against the doctor, against Jerome, against the very man who sheltered her.

Yet how could she apologize? How could she explain that she was only railing against Doc Greavy's ignorance of the tremendous advances medical science had made in treating mental illness in the past century?

Vera sighed. The irony of her situation was sadly laughable. It didn't matter what medical strides Doc Greavy did or didn't know about. She wasn't "confused" anyway; she was the victim of an inexplicable circumstance that a hundred years of bed rest wouldn't cure.

But how could she get back to her own time, her own people? The answer, she felt certain, was contained somewhere on the pages of Verity's journal. Only when she'd figured out how to purchase a one-way ticket back to the twentieth century could she hope to explain to Jericho.

Picking up the book once more, Vera started at the beginning and stepped into the life and dreams of the girl who'd influenced her own life for so many years.

October 20, 1896. I went with Rafe into town today. Mama's too close to the end of her confinement and I got to shop for the staples to see us through the winter. Buying flour and sugar and suchlike wasn't much fun, but Rafe left me at Pike's Store while he went to do some business. After we loaded the supplies I looked at all the new calico fabrics. I'd love to have a pretty dress made out of bright red calico. And a lacy petticoat peeking out beneath the hem. I'd twirl my skirts as I walked along the boardwalk and maybe somebody would ask me to the harvest dance they always have in Goodie Blenkenship's barn.

Rafe wouldn't let me go anyhow. And Mama says I need to stop worrying my mind about Mr. Jackson. She says he's too old for me and too worldly. Don't know what she means by that.

Anyway, the trip was fun. Until the ride home. Rafe must have done his business at one of the saloons. He was all liquored up and almost run us off the road more than once. Had to give him an elbow so's he'd keep his hands offen me.

But I love going to the city. All the ladies in

their fine clothes and the excitement in the air. Everyone seems in such a hurry.

Someday I'm going to the city for good. Won't no one ever talk me into living in a shack on a lonely mountainside like Mama.

Vera set the journal down. Verity seemed so young. So lonely. Would she ever realize her wish to live in the city—even a tiny little village like Jerome? On a more personal level, Vera wondered if she would ever get back to California. If she'd ever see her own apartment, her cat again. Maybe. If she and Verity both managed to survive these next few days they both might just see their dreams come true.

THAT EVENING Susannah Sweet, the barmaid with the fiery red hair nicknamed Sweet Sue by the men, brought up a dinner tray for Vera.

"What's the matter, honey? You feelin' poorly?" She uncovered a plate heaped with enough fried chicken and mashed potatoes to feed the entire mining town.

"What's he trying to do, fatten me up for the kill?"

Susannah gave her a quizzical glance. "Reckon Mr. Jackson just wants you to build up your strength. Seein's how you're so sickly. Ain't many men who'd treat a woman so special."

Feeling the sting of her gentle rebuke, Vera nodded. "You're right. I didn't mean anything except…it's really too much food. Can you join me?"

The barmaid's face lit with pleasure. "Thanks anyway, hon, but I've got to get back downstairs. Now that the posse's back there's plenty of thirsty men awaitin' my attention.''

Vera picked up a drumstick and bit into the crunchy coating. ''Mmm. Delicious. The posse. They, um, didn't find the girl's trail?''

''Nope, she's disappeared like a steam offen a hot kettle. Just gone.''

''Maybe it's for the best,'' Vera murmured as she forked up a healthy bite of potatoes.

''Reckon you're right at that. Ask me, the town's better off without that no-account Rafe Wilson anyway. Course, Sally don't agree. Rafe used to bring her lots of presents.''

''Sally?''

''The one with the bottle-yeller hair. Poker dealer. Her and Rafe was friends.''

''Really? I thought he was married.''

Susannah laughed, holding her arms across her stomach. ''Oh, honey, you're a pure pleasure. Since when has marriage stopped a man from bringing ribbons and bolts of fabric to a gal he fancies? For a gal who works in saloons, you're such an innocent.''

Innocent? No, but out of step with the times, yes. Once again Vera realized how flimsy was the fabric of her cover story. Sooner or later one of her slips was going to cause someone to ask questions. Questions she couldn't answer.

Wiping a bead of moisture from her eyes, Susannah patted Vera's arm. ''Well, gotta go, hon. You're a prize, you are.''

She started for the door and paused in midstride. ''Ooops. Almost forgot.'' Returning to the bedside, she pulled a small brown bottle from a pocket in her voluminous skirt. "Mr. Jackson says you're supposed to take this tonic the doctor ordered. Five drops in this glass of water."

Vera made a dismissive gesture. "Just set it down...I'll take it later. Probably just a placebo anyway."

"Don't know what a placebo is but Mr. Jackson said you was supposed to drink it now. Whilst I'm here, then I have to bring the bottle back to him."

"Oh, for crying out loud! I'm not a child, I'll take my medicine when I'm ready."

Susannah shook her head, her almost pretty features jutting in determination. "Nope. You gotta take it now. Else Mr. Jackson said he'd come up here and pour it down your gullet."

His attempt to intimidate her by threat would normally cause Vera to plant her feet and refuse the elixir—no matter how much she needed the medication. But the knowledge that she still owed Jericho an apology, combined with the quivery sensation that kept her off-kilter whenever he was nearby, was enough to make her capitulate. She'd deal with Jericho and these worthless patent medicines in the morning, after she'd finished Verity's journal and had a better idea how to proceed.

Shrugging with defeat, she flicked a thumb toward the water tumbler. "All right, fill her up."

Susannah carefully measured five drops of a vile-smelling green liquid. The water clouded and a virulent-looking scum floated on top.

Vera sniffed and drew back. "I'm not putting that stuff into my body. It might be lethal."

"Then I'll fetch Mr. Jackson."

With a growl, Vera snatched the glass from her hand and downed the contents. The potion tasted as venal as it looked and she quickly chased it with another bite of fried chicken.

The red-haired barmaid clucked with satisfaction and slipped the bottle of tonic back into her pocket. Vera could hear her chuckling as she closed the outside door.

Wiping her greasy fingers on the cloth napkin on the dinner tray, she poured a fresh glass of water and picked up Verity's journal.

February 19, 1896. The baby started coming the other night. It weren't like the other boys. This one come hard and was taking too long. Mama didn't want me to leave her so I had to send Tad to fetch the doctor. Seemed like forever before they got back. I was so worried.

Doc delivered the baby, another boy. His mouth was open and he was hollering, just like his daddy. But Mama was still sickly afterward. Doc told me to fetch Rafe.

Vera stifled a yawn. She'd spent so much time in bed that her body thought it was tired. What she needed was to go outside and jog a couple of miles. She smiled, imagining Jericho's expression if he found her racing through the packed dirt street. He'd have her committed on the spot.

It was hard to believe that only a few days ago she seriously considered him a lunatic—or worse. In such a short time he'd become such an important element in her life. So important, in fact, that it frightened her.

Rubbing her eyes, she pushed aside disturbing thoughts of Jericho and focused again on the journal.

I rode Bessie, the mule, up the mountain to the new mine only to find out that Rafe was over to the Balbriggan. Fellas said he was elk hunting. Nothing to do but go after him. Three more miles. Lordy, was it bitter cold. No snow, but the coldness near about froze my bones solid.

Course, Rafe wasn't there neither. Even looked in the old mine shaft. Nothing in there but creaky timbers and that old silver shoe. That's when the snow started coming down. Hard. Barely made it back to the line shaft. Had to stay all night and half the next day. Weren't much to eat but a couple scraps of hardtack the mice hadn't got to.

Couldn't leave Bessie in the storm so I brought her inside with me. Sure smelled bad in that old shack by morning.

Vera dropped the journal to her chest and yawned. Reading Verity's journal again was like taking a walk through history. So much hurt accepted so matter-of-factly. The girl's make-do attitude was a characteristic lost by so many of Vera's own generation.

Yet she couldn't help mourn Verity's lost innocence. She should have been courting boys, going to dances and choosing new dresses, not riding bone weary through the wintery nights in search of her drunken, no-good stepfather. How hard the girl's life was, going to bed hungry more times than not. Vera's nose wrinkled, yet she couldn't suppress a smile at the image of Verity sharing her humble lodgings with a mule.

Pressing back another yawn, Vera delved again into Verity's intriguing saga.

When I finally got back to the house yesterday, Rafe was waiting. Hollered at me 'cause I wasn't helping Mama and tried to hit me. Him being so drunk made it easy for me to get away but I had to lay low in the barn most of the day. I'm so tired of being cold, hungry and scared. Maybe one of these days I'll grab that silver shoe and just go away. Mama says it's dangerous but I don't know what could be worse than living here with Rafe. Although the new baby's real sweet.

The journal slid from Vera's fingers as a heavy lump congealed in her throat. That poor girl; living in the shadow of a bully like Rafe Wilson. She had to clear Verity's name so the young woman could live in peace with her mother's people. It was the only chance she had to lead a decent life. Vera frowned.

Where was the *real* Verity? Vera's eyes felt like they'd been cemented shut. She couldn't recall ever being so tired. She needed to think about Verity and her trek through the wilderness and about those silver shoes. Did the Apache have a similar legend to the Cinderella fairy tale?

If the silver slippers fit Verity, would she be swept away to a place where she'd find Chief Charming and life happily ever after? Vera sighed. There was so much she'd like to share with her young ancestor; despite Vera's own self-reliance, wasn't she, too, always looking—hoping—to meet her own Chief Charming?

And why did Jericho Jackson's visage leap to Vera's mind whenever she thought about happily-ever-after?

Well, fairy tales were myths and legends—not real life—and the sooner Vera got her own fairy tale shoved firmly into place the sooner she would be able to concentrate on getting out of this time. Alive, with any luck.

Unable to fend off sleep any longer, Vera blew out the lantern and drifted into a restive slumber, her dreams filled with barefoot girls and snow and silver slippers. And dark-eyed men who dressed in black.

IT WAS THE ICY WIND seeping into her bones that brought Vera to a state of near wakefulness. At first she thought the dream of Verity wandering lost in the snow had become too real. But the cold was too deep, too penetrating to be a dream.

Vera nestled deep beneath the heavy feather comforter. Her face was numb yet she felt strangely alert—even though her sand-filled eyes begged for more sleep.

What had awakened her? Had something in Verity's journal nudged her subconscious?

A sound, so slight she almost missed it, penetrated her sleepy fog. A mouse? Vera hated the furry little rodents. Eyes still closed, she listened intently for the scratching of tiny claws on the planked wood floor.

Something brushed against the foot of the bed.

Something much larger than a mouse, something huge. Human-size. Jericho? Willing her weary eyes to open, she stared into the darkness, trying to discern a shape, a reason for her awakening, out of the shadowy recesses.

There! Hadn't something moved in that corner? Something almost hidden in the shadow cast by the wardrobe.

Focusing intently until her eyes burned from the effort, Vera almost decided the movement was a leftover fragment of dream when she sensed another motion. This time she was certain; a large shape was half hidden in the recess beside the mahogany bureau.

"Jericho?" Her voice was a weak croak in the stillness.

No one answered yet, but she had the strong impression of another presence in the room. A malevolent presence that chilled her blood.

The curtain fluttered and another gust of frigid air swept through the bedroom. Vera absolutely remembered closing that window before climbing into bed. A native of Southern California, she wasn't accustomed to these crisp wintry nights.

Someone had opened the window.

Someone was here in the room with her. Waiting.

Fully awake now, Vera tried to remember where she'd tossed her backpack. Although she hadn't brought her service revolver with her, she'd thrown a canister of pepper spray into her knapsack at the last minute. A woman, even one well schooled in self-defense, traveling alone on long, empty stretches of desert highway needed a measure of protection.

If she could get her hands on that backpack...

It was safely tucked into the wardrobe, she remembered now.

The familiar click of a pistol being cocked reverberated like a kettledrum in the quiet room. Her heart leapt to her throat. Chilled blood raced through her veins.

The intruder was going to shoot her!

The thought barely formed in her mind as Vera instinctively threw herself off the bed and landed with a painful thump on the hardwood floor. At the same moment, a gunshot blasted the air.

She rolled under the bed, scuffling to hide herself from the mad gunman, her senses recording every movement, every sound, like a slow-motion camera, preserving the horrifying events for eternity: The harsh, guttural sound of labored breathing as the killer came ever closer. Heavy footsteps pounding on the pine plank flooring in the other room. Shouts from far away. Her own heart, beating so wildly she feared her blood vessels wouldn't stand the pressure.

Suddenly, the bedroom door burst open.

"Vera! Are you all—" Jericho's voice broke as another gunshot rang out.

She heard a cry of pain—Jericho?—then a grunt

The Harlequin Reader Service® — Here's how it works:

Accepting your 2 free books and mystery gift places you under no obligation to buy anything. You may keep the books and gift and return the shipping statement marked "cancel." If you do not cancel, about a month later we'll send you 4 additional novels and bill you just $3.34 each in the U.S., or $3.71 in Canada, plus 25¢ delivery per book and applicable taxes if any.* That's the complete price and — compared to the cover price of $3.99 in the U.S. and $4.50 in Canada — it's quite a bargain! You may cancel at any time, but if you choose to continue, every month we'll send you 4 more books, which you may either purchase at the discount price or return to us and cancel your subscription.

*Terms and prices subject to change without notice. Sales tax applicable in N.Y. Canadian residents will be charged applicable provincial taxes and GST.

NO POSTAGE
NECESSARY
IF MAILED
IN THE
UNITED STATES

BUSINESS REPLY MAIL

FIRST-CLASS MAIL   PERMIT NO. 717   BUFFALO, NY

POSTAGE WILL BE PAID BY ADDRESSEE

HARLEQUIN READER SERVICE
3010 WALDEN AVE
PO BOX 1867
BUFFALO NY 14240-9952

If offer card is missing write to: Harlequin Reader Service, 3010 Walden Ave., P.O. Box 1867, Buffalo NY 14240-1867

Play The Lucky Hearts Game

and get...
FREE BOOKS, a FREE GIFT... and MUCH more!

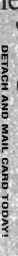

and the sounds of a struggle. Muffled curses punctuated the fight as bodies hit, flailed and thumped against the wall.

Then, a crashing sound at the window, as glass shattered, showering the room with clinking shards.

The room suddenly flooded with light and she peeked from under the bed. A dozen pairs of feet, booted, bare and clad in holey socks, milled around the small bedroom. The owners of those feet all seemed to be talking at once. The once silent bedchamber rang with chaotic voices.

Feeling safe at last, Vera slid from beneath the bed and stood up on wobbly knees. Several people had brought candlesticks and lanterns and a flickering golden glow bathed the room. Blinking against the brightness, Vera looked around for the one face she needed to see.

The one face that was missing.

As the miners gathered around her, asking a hundred questions at once, her bare foot touched something warm and moist.

Where was Jericho, she wondered as she glanced down.

A sharp pain, fed by nausea, filled her stomach.

She was standing in a pool of bright red blood.

Chapter Nine

Casting wildly about, Vera pushed aside Jess Wiggins and two other miners who were bent over a rumpled heap on the floor in front of the bureau.

"Jericho! Oh my God, are you—" her voice broke off as she stared in mute horror. Still as death, Jericho's blanched face was all but hidden by the smear of scarlet seeping from his hairline.

Dropping to her knees beside him, Vera shouted to the stunned crowd, "Someone get the doctor! Quick."

"I'll fetch him, though I suspect we're too late," Jess Wiggins said.

In response Vera ripped open Jericho's blood-stained shirt and laid her head on his chest. Gesturing for quiet, she listened intently for the reassuring beat of his heart. For a moment she heard nothing. *Come on, come on,* she prayed. *Beat, damn you, beat!*

Relief poured over her like a warm bath on a winter night as his strong, steady heartbeat thumped its reassurance against her ear.

A gush of hot tears filled her eyes and Vera swiped them away with the back of her hand. Relief that a human hadn't died, she told herself. Nothing more. To distract herself from the maelstrom of emotions whirling inside her, she looked up and spied Yorkie. "There's a basin of water on that nightstand. Bring it to me."

The shy young man darted to do her bidding.

Spotting Susannah Sweet's bright red hair, Vera called out, "Bring some towels. Hurry."

When they hurried back with the items she'd requested, Vera dipped a corner of rough toweling in the pan of tepid water and sponged the blood from Jericho's face. His eyes fluttered open. He blinked twice and wordlessly reached up to caress her cheek.

The raspy feel of his work-roughened fingertips felt like the finest silk against her skin. Biting her lip against the flood of emotion that moved like molten fire through her veins, Vera's trembling fingers returned to their task.

"I'm okay," he whispered. He started to sit up, then groaned and grabbed his head.

"Lay still!" she commanded, bundling a clean towel beneath his head and gently pressing him onto his back. Her voice was hoarse and quavery. She still couldn't quite believe that the horrendous-looking wound hadn't proved fatal.

A brusque voice cut through the gaggle of hushed murmurs. "Move aside, let me in. Pete, move the hell outta the way, will you?"

Doc Greavy knelt beside her. "What have we got here—a lovers' quarrel?"

The miners chittered appreciatively and Vera fought down a biting retort. She cared little for the doctor's dry frontier humor—it always seemed at her expense. "He's been shot," she said tightly.

The medic's blunt fingers probed Jericho's scalp, eliciting a cringe of pain from the wounded man. After a moment, Greavy rocked back on his heels. "Shot at, maybe. But only grazed. Get up, Jackson, and fetch me a beer. You'll live."

Jericho grunted. "Not unless I find a better sawbones." Reaching up for Jess Wiggins's helping hand, he rose to his feet. Taking the damp towel from Vera's limp hand, he wiped his face and tossed the used towel on the floor. He cast a rueful glance at the bedroom window, the white curtains flapping against the frosty air. "Reckon he got away."

"Who?" Wiggins strode to the window and stared down at the empty street. "Ain't nobody out here."

"Maybe he's hiding," Yorkie Delong added.

"Yeah, like your brain's hiding," Wiggins snorted to the amused snickers of the onlookers.

With Vera holding tight to Jericho's arm, they followed Wiggins to the window. A narrow balcony made a complete circle around the frame structure just below the second-story windows. Obviously, the would-be killer had used the veranda to effect his entry—and his escape.

She sagged against Jericho's firm chest. "I thought he'd killed you," she whispered, oblivious to the crowd and the danger of being exposed for who she really was. Oblivious to everything but the sick feeling of near loss trumpeting through her breast.

Jericho reached down and knuckled a silky strand of ink black hair from her eyes. He felt like kicking something. If he had half the sense of a billy goat, he should've anticipated an attempt on her life. It was just fool's luck that Vera hadn't been killed. Obviously, someone had seen through her disguise, even if the men currently in this room didn't seem to. Unfortunately, the same someone who'd shot Rafe Wilson in the back wouldn't balk at killing a woman. Although the attack on Vera wouldn't clear her reputation insofar as the general population was concerned, it was proof enough for Jericho that her altercation with her stepfather ended with a whack from a cast iron skillet. The real killer must have taken advantage of Rafe's unconscious state to finish him off. At the same time, shifting the blame to Rafe's innocent stepdaughter.

Justice had failed to protect her, and now Jericho, too, had failed to keep her safe. He swore it wouldn't happen again.

Wiggins turned away from the window and smirked, a gap-toothed grin that held no humor. "Looks like the bandit got clean away. Iffen he ever existed, that is."

Jericho released Vera and stepped forward until he stood jaw-to-jaw with the quarrelsome miner. "What's that supposed to mean?"

Wiggins shrugged, his broad shoulders nearly touching his ears. "Just sayin', that's all."

A new voice boomed over the buzzing crowd. "Why don't you tell us exactly what happened here, Mr. Jackson?"

Jericho turned from Wiggins and grasped Deputy Hamblin's beefy hand. "Good to see you back,

Henry. Can't tell you much except I heard a gunshot and ran in here to find some scalawag fixin' to shoot Miz, er, LaFleur here.''

Deputy Hamblin nodded to Vera. "Ah, Miz La-Fleur, I've been hearing a lot about you."

She looked up at the gray-haired, brawny lawman who'd apparently led the unsuccessful search for Verity. She cringed at the assessing look in his cold blue eyes.

"Hope you weren't hearing bad reviews," she quipped in an attempt to keep him focused on her stage persona.

"No, ma'am, I understand you're quite a songstress. The boys say your performance is terrific. So, what exactly happened here?"

Vera glanced around at the gaggle of intent watchers. She was hesitant to tell her story in front of the entire town because of her fear that someone would make the connection between the attack on her life and her more apparent resemblance to Verity Mc-Bride.

Picking up on her hesitation, and perhaps mistaking it for modesty, Deputy Hamblin turned to the onlookers. "Say, fellas, I appreciate y'all coming around to lend a hand, but I need to take Miz LaFleur's statement so why don't you all head on back downstairs?"

At their grumbling response, Jericho raised a hand. "Just a minute! Miz LaFleur and I *are* grateful for all your help and to show our appreciation, the house wants to buy all of you a drink. But that offer's good only for the next ten minutes."

The small crowd didn't need more encouragement.

The quicker men moved en masse through the narrow doorway, nearly trampling the slower moving men in their gleeful anticipation. In a matter of seconds, the room was cleared, leaving only the deputy, Jericho and Vera behind.

Hamblin nodded at Vera's nightshirt. "So, you must have been in bed when the ruckus started?"

Vera glanced down. Seeing her scandalously exposed legs, she felt the color rise in her face. "Oh, goodness, excuse me for a moment, please."

As if he, too, had just noticed her bare limbs, Jericho took the deputy by the elbow. "Maybe we'd better conduct our visit in the parlor. Can I offer you a drop of brandy, Henry?"

"The good stuff?"

"My pleasure."

When the two men stepped into the front room, Vera sagged onto the bed. She hadn't realized what an emotional toll the evening's experience had taken on her. She was so tired she felt as if she could crawl beneath the covers and hibernate for the next full month. No doubt, Doc's elixir—however weak—was having some effect.

Dragging herself to the closet, she donned the only respectable garment she owned, a blue calico day dress that Jericho had purchased for her at Morgan's Mercantile. After a quick swipe at her hair, she dabbed a cloth in water and wiped the sleep from her eyes. Maybe she could stay awake another five minutes. She yawned. Maybe.

Opening the bedroom door she joined the two men who rose to their feet when she entered the room.

There were some things about living in the past that she liked; the reverence most good men felt for women, for instance.

Taking the settee for her wide skirt, she smiled and nodded at the men, their cue to sit again. Slowly, she was learning the rules of the frontier social structure.

The deputy sat on the straight-backed, horsehair chair kitty-corner to the sofa. Jericho crossed the room to slide onto the settee beside Vera. She moved her voluminous skirt to accommodate him, grateful for the open endorsement of his close proximity.

When everyone was settled, Henry Hamblin smiled at her. "Feelin' better, Miz LaFleur?"

"Thank you, deputy. Yes, I am."

"Then let me ask you some questions, see if we can catch this varmint. Jericho says you woke up and felt like somebody was in the room with you?"

She hesitated, recalling that awful moment when she knew someone had broken into her room. As if sensing her distress, Jericho's hand slipped beneath the folds of her cotton skirt to clasp hers. Buoyed by his unflagging support, she pushed aside the raw emotions evoked by the memory and raised her chin. "That's right. I couldn't actually see him but I sensed he was there."

Hamblin stared at her for a long time before speaking. "Kind of like your instincts were honed, looking for danger, is that right?"

"I guess you could say that."

"Then this intruder—'cause if I understand right, nobody actually saw him—that so?"

"No, I never saw his face," she said.

The deputy looked to Jericho for confirmation. He shook his head. "I had a sense of a large man, but there was no light in the room, no moonlight, and, frankly, he took me by surprise. I heard a shot, raced in and was hit in the belly soon's I came in the doorway."

"That's when he shot you—while you were on the ground?"

"Yeah, like the yellow-bellied lizard that he is." Jericho gingerly touched the fiery gash along his temple.

"I see." Hamblin turned his attention back to Vera. "This man must've been watching you for some time for you to…feel it and wake up."

"I suppose," she responded, wondering where he was heading with his odd questions.

"And yet you believed he wasn't there to, um, force his attentions on you?"

Slowly tossing her head, Vera considered his question. "No. This was no overly ardent admirer. He intended to kill me."

Hamblin leaned back on the rigid chair and stared into her eyes. "Now why do you suppose that was, Miz LaFleur? I mean, I've been an Arizona Ranger for more years than I care to count and I have to tell you, I've never met up with a fellow who had such an unnatural bent as to want to kill a beautiful woman."

He twisted his head to face Jericho and continued in a conversational tone. "Have you ever heard of such a thing?"

Before Jericho could reply, the deputy continued

his verbal speculation. "No sir, it don't seem natural. Now I've seen family squabbles that got out of hand and someone died, and I've seen ladies kilt because of jealous rages, but I've never known of a man to sneak into a woman's bedchamber with the pure purpose of wanting to kill her."

A dead silence filled the air as Vera tried to think of a response. In her time, women murdered in their beds were an all too common occurrence. It was refreshing to realize the law in Jerome found such crimes remarkable.

Yet, without exposing her own secret, how could she explain that the would-be killer had ample reason to wish her dead? No doubt, whoever had attacked her thought she was Verity—and the only person who knew someone other than herself was guilty of Rafe's murder.

Jericho cleared his voice. "Maybe the man *did* attack out of jealous rage. Maybe he saw her onstage, thought she was singing to him and built up a story in his mind that she was…was his. Then, if he saw her come into my room…maybe that provoked him."

Hamblin tapped his fingers against his bearded chin as he considered the explanation. "Maybe so, Jericho. That might be an acceptable explanation 'cept for one thing."

"And what's that?" Jericho ran his fingertip along the rim of the brandy snifter and polished off the golden dregs.

Vera could see Jericho was trying to act nonchalant, as if the motive behind the attack would turn out to be some acceptable masculine failing. But his fear—and hers—was almost palpable in the still room. Henry Hamblin was edging too close to the truth.

The deputy set his empty snifter on a small table and leaned forward, elbows propped on his knees, his chin resting between his thumbs. "From what the boys tell me, Miz LaFleur's only been in town a couple days. Don't seem likely that a man would get all het up about a woman he's only seen once or twice."

He raised a hand to forestall Jericho's objection. "No, no. Let me finish. Now I'll grant you a woman as handsome as Miz LaFleur here could engender some powerful emotions in a man, if you'll forgive the personal reference, ma'am?"

Vera nodded, not trusting her voice to speak.

"But it seems there's a much more likely explanation," Hamblin continued.

Again silence filled the room until the tension was as real and edgy as the fear she'd felt waiting for news outside the mine after the accident. The gentle ticktock of the grandfather clock in the corner was as loud as the tolling of doom.

Finally, Jericho broke the quiet. "And that other explanation, Henry?"

"Well, seems more simple if we was to accept the fact that Vera LaFleur probably ain't this purty lady's real name. Is it, ma'am?"

Vera sat stock still, not answering, barely daring to breathe.

"Now I may be a little slow, but my eyesight ain't give out yet. Reckon your costume and all that fald-erol you painted your face with might have fooled the men, but, ma'am, you ain't wearing no face paint now and the answer's clear as the nose on your purty face. You're Verity McBride or my name ain't Henry Makepeace Hamblin.''

"DON'T RECKON we'll need the handcuffs, will we ma'am?''

Recognizing the deputy was asking for her word that she wouldn't attempt to escape custody, Vera shook her head. "No, I'll go peacefully.''

"The hell you will!'' Jericho slammed the flat of his hand against the solid wood door. Whirling around he jammed his hands on his hips and glared at Hamblin. "You're sentencing her to death and you expect her to just give in and go quietly?''

"There'll be a trial, Jackson. Ain't going to be no lynching in my jurisdiction.''

Jericho laughed, a harsh guttural noise that told Vera just how desperate he believed her situation to be. "A trial? You must be joking. When the hell has anyone with Indian blood ever received a fair trial in this territory?''

Seeing Vera's stubborn look, Jericho added, "Guess we don't have much choice, do we? If she doesn't give herself up to the law, they'll just put a bounty on her head.''

He hated to frighten her even more, but he had to make her understand the seriousness of the situation. Now that she'd been found out, a cell in Prescott was the only place she'd be safe.

Hamblin placed a calming hand on Jericho's shoulder. "I don't think you're giving folks hereabouts much credit. Everyone knows Rafe Wilson was meaner than a cornered rattler, and that'll count some with the jury. And Miz McBride and her mother are pretty respected in this town. My missus still talks about the time she stayed up all night nursing our youngun through the fever.''

"Yeah, but your missus can't serve on the jury," Jericho retorted.

Suddenly, Vera understood his very real concern about a jury trial. This was the late nineteenth century, Arizona was still a territory and women didn't yet have the right to vote. That meant the working men of Jerome, Rafe's cronies and drinking buddies, would comprise the jury of Verity's ''peers.''

A cold sickness swept through Vera, and she rocked from the realization of her true peril. "Wh-what about a change of venue?''

"Say what?'' Hamblin's grizzled gray eyebrows furrowed in confusion.

"What are the chances of moving the trial to a larger city? Someplace where Rafe's friends won't serve on the jury.''

"Ah. Well now, I don't see why not. Jerome ain't got a courthouse or even a judge. We'd have to wait for the circuit judge to come around next month anyhow. No reason not to just take you down to the county seat. Might be better all around.''

"County seat?'' She hated to expose more of her ignorance of her surroundings, but he could be talking about Cottonwood or Phoenix.

Jericho's concerned glance told her information was being conveyed that she should already know.

"Prescott's the seat of Yavapai County, Ver. Most official business is conducted there."

She nodded. "Will I have the benefit of a lawyer?"

"Of course!" Hamblin snorted. "Where do you think you are—in some lawless outpost of civilization?"

Henry Hamblin's good-ole-boy facade was merely that, she realized with a start. Underneath his shucks-howdy exterior, an intelligent, educated man was in complete control. She'd do well to remember not to underestimate him again in the future.

Raising her chin, she stepped forward. "All right. When do we leave for Prescott?"

"First thing in the mornin'."

"That means I'll have to spend the night in jail."

Jericho and Hamblin exchanged a glance. The deputy cleared his throat and stared with entirely too much attention to a porcelain figurine on the occasional table. "Er, uh, no, not exactly."

Crossing the small room to stand in front of her, Jericho took her shoulders in his firm grasp. "Jerome doesn't have a jail."

"Oh." She sighed, relieved that she wouldn't have to spend the rest of the night on a urine-soaked cement-floored cell.

Her sense of relief was short-lived when she recalled that uneasy glance they'd exchanged. A sick curiosity forced her to ask, "Where do you house the prisoners before taking them to Prescott for trial?"

Hamblin picked up the porcelain figurine to study it in even greater detail. "Uh, we, um, usually just handcuff 'em to a, er, wagon wheel or something."

"What!"

She couldn't believe her ears. Into what kind of barbarous society had she fallen prey? "You mean you just leave people tied up in the street like dogs? Overnight?"

Hamblin frowned and slowly nodded. "Most of our prisoners are just drunks who need to sleep it off anyhow. If it's raining or cold like tonight, though, we usually shackle them to a wagon inside the livery stable."

How much worse was this nightmare going to become before she finally woke up? Or before she finally regained her old life? Suddenly, the tiny one-bedroom apartment she shared with Squiggles, her tabby cat, seemed like the safest haven on earth. If she got out of this mess Vera vowed never again to complain about lonely weekends and a boring life. Boring wasn't all that bad.

While the nausea boiled in her stomach, she at last found her voice, although she could barely force out more than a whisper. "So, I'm to spend the night bound to a wagon wheel and left in an unheated barn?"

Hamblin laughed uneasily. "Now that you talk on it, it don't seem right. Reckon I'll have to make other arrangements. If we didn't have Missus Hamblin's sister from Saint Louis staying with us, I'd put you up at our place."

"Why can't she just spend the rest of the night here?" Jericho asked as he released Vera's shoulders.

Hamblin hesitated. "Don't know that she'd be safe here, once word gets out."

"If you don't tell, how will anyone know?" Jericho asked reasonably.

"I have to wire the sheriff in Prescott. You know full well that Marvin Shott's a terrible gossip. Minute I hand him the telegram and take my leave he'll run to the nearest saloon and spread the word."

Jericho raised his head and stared at the deputy. "She'll be safe here. I'll see to it." He flipped back the edge of his long black jacket, exposing the pearl-handled Colt .44 holstered to his thigh.

Hamblin rubbed his chin. "And I have your word Miz McBride will be here in the mornin'? Ready to travel to Prescott?"

Jericho nodded. "You have my word."

Vera collapsed onto the settee. Just like that they'd settled her fate. It never occurred to either of them to ask her how she felt about her own sleeping arrangements. Although to be fair she'd obviously already been in accord with a similar plan. Still, she had to accept the fact that she was in another time, one where women had no real say about their fate. She'd fallen into a world she didn't understand and couldn't cope with yet. At this point, the best she could hope for was the freedom to live out her life in this unenlightened and hostile world.

Chapter Ten

Deputy Hamblin finally left after obtaining Jericho's word that Vera wouldn't be left alone. Jericho closed the door behind him and exhaled a deep, ragged sigh of frustration.

He'd repaid his debt to Min-e-wah by placing her only daughter in jeopardy. Instead of taking her directly to the Apache village as he should've done, he'd made the unilateral decision that she needed medical help and insisted she accompany him back to Jerome. A decision that might now cost her life.

A few days ago, her biggest problem had been defending herself against Rafe Wilson's drunken rages. Now, thanks to Jericho, she also had to worry about Rafe's killer, a bloodthirsty lynch mob and a racially biased jury. Good job, Jackson.

He turned from the door, finally ready to face her accusing eyes.

The dark eyes that met his gaze, however, were meltingly soft, almost heartbreaking in their obvious trust. The cold shell that had tightly bound his heart for so many years thawed like the last snowflake under a bright spring sun.

Crossing the room, he paused before drawing her into his arms. "I can't tell you how sorry I am," he whispered into her soft hair.

"It's not your fault," she murmured. She was stiff, unyielding for a heartbeat before melting against him.

His fingers clenched convulsively, drawing her so close he thought her bones would surely penetrate his flesh. "It's *all* my fault. If I hadn't been so pigheaded, so sure I was right—"

She drew back and pressed a fingertip against his lips. "Shhh. I believe in the system, Jericho. I've always championed following rules and operating within the bounds of the law. I can't abandon that faith now or my whole life will have been a sham."

He couldn't believe she was so ready to let him off the hook. He didn't deserve amnesty, and he didn't deserve to have a woman like Vera in his arms. Unable to release his own guilt so easily, he once more sought to shoulder the blame. "I should've taken you to the Apache encampment as soon as I pulled you out of that mine shaft."

Vera smiled gently. "That was the first time you saved my life. But, Jericho, I've never lived among the Apache. The world I know has always been the…white world. No, this is where I need to prove my innocence. That wasn't a mistake. You've shown me nothing but kindness."

Kindness? No, his behavior wasn't predicated by kindness. Guilt, yes. Repayment of a debt, yes. Stubbornness, yes. And lust, hell yes. But he couldn't allow her to credit him with a grace of spirit he didn't possess.

Vera wouldn't listen to another word. Taking his hand, she led the way to the settee. "Please don't ask me to explain now, Jericho, but there are so many things I need to know. Things…things I should already know. Will you help me?"

"Of course," he said without thinking. He couldn't remember another occasion in his life when someone asked for his help with such sincerity, such appealing guilelessness. A dozen times a week someone needed money, or free drinks, or asked him to lend his name to some fund-raising event, but to need *him?* His counsel and his physical help? This was a new and disarming experience.

Jericho Jackson grew up in saloons, spent his early teens on Mississippi paddle wheelers. He'd never known his mother; his father wouldn't talk about her and Jericho never even knew whether she was alive or dead. Yet he missed the softness of a woman's gentle guidance.

Oh, his father had tried to do his best for the boy, but Martin Jackson had been a professional gambler. He'd hauled young Jericho from one saloon to the next. While he was good to the boy—there was always ample food, warm clothing and shelter—Martin Jackson wouldn't, or couldn't, offer the affection Jericho so badly needed.

It was always, "Boy, help sweep up the kitchen," or "Boy, fetch me and the fellers a drink," or, "Boy, it's time you went upstairs now." On the infrequent occasions when his father brought one of the dance hall girls back to his room, young Jericho was expected to make himself scarce until morning.

Those were the times Jericho loved the most. He'd go back downstairs to the raucous gambling hall and study the card sharks at work. Most were eager to show off for the young admirer and introduced him to the secrets of professional card playing. They'd taught young Jericho more than when to hold and when to fold. They'd taught him to keep his expression blank, his emotions hidden deep inside, and to keep his own counsel. The same rules he'd used to govern his life for most of his thirty-three years.

Rules that hadn't worked since he first heard Vera's plaintiff voice calling from that mine shaft.

Rules that weren't working now.

Now he tried to put aside his raw awareness of that tiny little hollow at the base of her throat. The sweetly scented spot that pulsed with her lifeblood.

As if oblivious to his sudden and nearly over-whelming need, Vera spoke quietly. "I need to know about the trial. How does it work?"

Dragged back to the problems that threatened to overwhelm them both, he shrugged. "They'll find you a lawyer, pick a jury and there'll be a trial."

She tossed her head, flyaway strands of ebony floating through the air like errant silken webs. "What about proof? I mean, if no one saw Ver— Er, the murder committed, how can they positively prove who killed Rafe?"

"Everybody knows you two fought worse than a weasel and a snake."

"Which am I?" she asked ruefully. "The weasel or the snake?"

Jericho turned to face her, sorry for the offhand

choice of words that had offended her. "Neither. I'd say you were an...angel caught in a war between the devil and his minions."

She nodded slowly. "Yeah, I kind of feel like the devil is dancing on my petticoats right now. But back to the trial. They can't have any forensic evidence or—"

"What's forensic evidence?"

"You know, rifling marks on the bullet, finger-prints, DNA, trace evidence, that sort of thing—"

At his bewildered expression, she broke off and said, "Oh. You don't have that kind of scientific ability yet, do you? I keep forgetting where I am."

Jericho scratched his head. "Ver, sweetie, I know you don't think Doc Greavy's got much on the ball, but...but I don't know what in hell you're talking about."

Tears filled her eyes and Jericho thought he might drown in their sudden sadness. "Never mind. It was just something I once read about."

She tried to blink away the moisture filming her eyes. Turning quickly away, she stared out the window into the black night.

He'd never had a woman up and break into tears before. The women in Jericho's life were hardened, toughened by the rough existence they had to muck out of the wilderness. Vera's tears eroded the calluses of indifference that had long since formed over his heart.

Reaching into his coat pocket for the dress kerchief he always carried, he dabbed her eyes. "Now, don't go crying on me. Get mad, yell at me, hit me, hell I deserve it! Kick the living bejeebers out of me. Just don't cry.''

"But...but don't you see? It's hopeless! How can I possibly prove I *didn't* kill Rafe Wilson? That's why our founding fathers set up our rights the way they did—innocent until proven guilty. So with no witnesses and no real evidence, how could a jury find me guilty beyond a reasonable doubt? Yet that's exactly what's going to happen and I can't stop it!''

Unable to bear the sight of her heartbreak any longer, Jericho wrapped his arms around her, pressing her damp face against his chest. "I don't know what it's going to take to prove your innocence, but we're going to do it! You've got to trust me now."

She drew back and looked into his eyes. "I...I don't have any choice, Jericho. You're all I've got."

The enormity of her words filled him with a warm, heated glow that seemed to emanate from low in his stomach, spreading out to singe his limbs and scorch his heart. His entire life, until this moment, had been a solitary, empty existence.

Until Vera reached deep into his soul and touched him with a sweet, golden intimacy so freely given. "Don't do that," he growled, unable to bear the burden of her unqualified faith in his less-than-sterling character. "Don't put that kind of responsibility on my shoulders." *Or that kind of trust.*

"The only thing I'm asking of you," she whispered, "is that you don't abandon me. Don't leave me to face this alone."

Fear and uncertainty melted into physical, primal need. Utter, churning, demanding want for this woman filled his belly. He pulled her into his arms. His mouth lowered to capture hers, soft, yielding and filled with an urgency as raw and compelling as his own.

She sank against him with a mew of surprise mingled with unabashed delight. Her full, womanly breasts pressed against his chest, their sweet pressure almost unendurable.

Groaning with his raging desire, Jericho traced his hands down her shoulders, brushing against her form-defining bodice until he found those rounded hills of enchantment.

Jericho was bombarded with emotions he'd never imagined. He was a man who'd experienced much. No stranger to the charms of a woman's body, he was powerless against the hot tide surging in his loins. But this was more than mere physical yearning. This was the ancient need of a man to claim a woman as his own. To give himself fully, unreservedly, to this woman in return.

Dropping his head, he delighted in her murmur of pleasure as his tongue sought and taunted her nipple through the cottony fabric. Jericho wanted nothing more than to spend this night—and eternity—exploring her seductive body. Giving pleasure instead of taking it for his own.

Slowly, though, another dimension of reality faded into his awareness. In the distance, almost hidden by his intensity, Jericho became aware of the hum of excited voices.

He paused in his ardent ministrations, wondering if he'd mistaken the roar of his heated blood for the voices he heard. No, the voices were closer now. Louder.

"What's that?" Vera's frightened voice broke the spell.

He pulled away and stood up, turning his back in order to hide the evidence of his arousal while he buttoned his thigh-length black coat. In a voice unfamiliar in its raspiness, he replied, "I'd better go check."

But before he could reach the door to the corridor, the hum of voices strengthened to a strident, piercing clamor. Placing his palm on his pistol butt, he threw open the door.

Led by Jess Wiggins, a crowd of about twenty men tromped down the hallway in his direction.

"Where is she? You're hiding that murderin' little bitch and we want her," Wiggins, the self-appointed spokesman, demanded.

The mob roared their agreement. In the back, almost looking ashamed, Jericho spotted Yorkie watching intently.

Sensing Vera cross the room to see what was happening, Jericho moved into the corridor, closing the door firmly behind him. Flipping the tails of his jacket behind his hip, exposing his Colt, he stepped forward until his chest was inches from Wiggins's.

Fetid fumes from the miner's alcohol breath soured the air between them.

Jericho waited until the mob stilled before he said quietly, "I know you weren't referring to Miz La-Fleur in such a crude manner."

Still filled with the bravado of a liquor-filled belly

and a gallery of appreciative disciples, Wiggins puffed his chest out until it slammed into Jericho's. ''And so what if I am?''

''Then I wouldn't take kindly to it....'' Without warning, Jericho drew back and punched Wiggins in the stomach.

''Whuuf!'' The larger man bent over and clutched his midriff, trying without much success to suck oxygen back into his pain-wracked body.

''And I'd have to teach you better manners,'' Jericho concluded, stepping back, his fist still cocked.

Gagging and choking from the force of the blow, Wiggins staggered backward and looked up at Jericho with bleary eyes. ''What'd ya have to go and do that for?''

''Because you need to learn to keep a civil tongue in that foul mouth of yours, my friend.''

Wiggins drew back his fist. ''Why, I oughta—''

''Think very carefully before you act,'' Jericho intoned, his dark eyebrows raised like warning flags. ''Because next time I won't stop until your sorry butt's lying in a worthless heap at the bottom of those stairs.''

Darting a glance over his shoulder at the steep staircase, Wiggins hesitated. ''How come you want to take up for a murderin' flooz—'' he paused, catching Jericho's thunderous glare. ''I mean, why'd ya wanta take up for a killer like that?''

Taking advantage of the man's cowardly nature, Jericho strode forward, invading Wiggins's space, knowing the deliberate action would make Jess look bad in front of his followers. He knew he couldn't take on all twenty men if they got out of hand, but if he could cut the head off this angry snake, Jericho thought he might stand a chance of saving Vera's life.

He grabbed the big man's dirty red plaid shirt. "We're not having any mob justice, Wiggins. The sheriff's taking her to Prescott for trial and a jury will decide whether or not she killed Rafe Wilson. But I'll be damned if I'm going to let you—" he paused and scanned the crowd, giving each man a full two seconds of his cold rage "—and your drunken friends take the law into your own hands."

"But everyone knows—"

"Knows what?" Jericho demanded. He turned to Hank Peters, normally a mild-mannered man, although easily led. "How about you, Pete? You know for sure, deep in your heart, that she shot Rafe Wilson in the back? You see her do it?"

"Uh, no. Course not."

"How about you, Greenblatt? You willing to bet your own life that she's guilty?"

The thin proprietor of the only cafe in town shook his head. "Naw, Jericho. But...but Wiggins said—"

Swinging back around, Jericho released his hold on Jess Wiggins. The burly miner spun through the hallway and landed against the far wall. The entire building shook in his wake. "Since when did you all set such store by Jess Wiggins's great intelligence? When did you all give up your belief in following the law? In exacting justice?"

Now their heads were drooping; no one would look directly into Jericho's eyes. Dropping his voice, he drew on every negotiating skill he'd ever learned.

"You've all been drinking my liquor and playing cards with me for years. Any of you ever know me to break my word?"

All twenty heads popped up.

"Naw," Greenblatt spoke first. "You never broke your word far's I know."

"Me, neither," Hank Peters agreed.

"How about you, Yorkie? Or you Mariton? Any of you ever hear of me not keeping a promise?"

When no one answered in the affirmative, Jericho continued. "Then I'll make this promise now. You fellas all go on back downstairs and play a friendly round of poker. Or, better yet, go on home to your wives. Let the law handle this and I promise that Verity McBride will have her day in court. And that ought to be enough for any of you."

Yorkie stepped forward. "It's enough for me, Mr. Jackson."

Hat in hand, he edged back down the steps.

One by one they followed until only Jess Wiggins, still huddled on the floor against the wall, was left. He stared up at Jericho, hatred glittering in his mud-colored eyes. "All right, have it your way for now, Jackson. But mark my words, that bi—woman's going to swing for my friend's murder."

Not as long as I have breath flowing through my body, Jericho silently vowed. He'd break the law, his word and his body to keep Vera from the hangman's noose. By God he would.

Biting his upper lip to keep from punching the vengeful bastard in his big mouth, Jericho said quietly, "Go on back to the bar, Wiggins. It's over for tonight."

Swiping a bead of moisture from his upper lip, Wiggins slowly regained his feet and made his unsteady way down the stairs.

Jericho breathed in relief. Somehow he'd pulled it off. He'd managed to fend off a mob hungry for revenge. Could he do it again? Would he have to?

Jericho turned around.

Vera was standing in the doorway, a heavy cast iron poker clenched in her hand. Tears glimmered, unshed, in her eyes. God, she looked wonderful. A strong, spirited warrior ready to defend herself—and him, he had no doubt—against all comers. He'd never been so proud of anyone in his life.

Swallowing the lump in his throat, Jericho crossed the short distance and took the fireplace implement from her tightly drawn fist. "It's over," he whispered, kissing her lightly on the temple.

She looked up at him, her dark eyes filled with unbearable pain. "Is it really? I don't think this nightmare will ever end."

He reached for her but she pulled away. "That's the second time you've saved my life. Thank you."

Head held suspiciously high, she turned and swept back into his apartment.

Jericho took a deep breath and followed. He hoped he wouldn't have to test his luck a third time. But he wouldn't bet on it.

Chapter Eleven

Vera didn't think she'd ever be able to sleep. Still, she must have dozed off at some point during the endless night because she was startled awake by Jericho's hand gently shaking her shoulder. "Time to get up. Deputy Hamblin's here."

His bleak visage reminded her that even though she'd awakened from sleep, she was still trapped in the nightmare.

She sat up and stared around the dim room. The first faint signs of gray were just starting to light the eastern sky. The room was bitterly cold, and she clutched the comforter under her chin. Jericho was busying himself gathering her things from the wardrobe. He kept his back turned, as if he couldn't bear to face her.

Vera understood. She could hardly face looking into the mirror and seeing herself. A few short days ago she'd been a content, if not happy, woman. She'd enjoyed a fairly fulfilling career as a patrol officer, had a nice apartment that she'd slowly filled with comfy Americana antiques, a cat she adored, and a few good friends.

There had been room for improvement, of course. A change in career path, for example, that would include the more investigative processes in law enforcement. Lately her nesting antennae had been quivering and a special man in her life would have been an added bonus. And even though her mother's losing battle with Alzheimer's overshadowed all her petty grievances, Vera had long resigned herself to the fact that the woman she'd known as her mother was gone; replaced by this stranger who didn't even recognize her.

Now, only a few days later, that old comfortable life was over. Today her jailer was transporting her to a small town in the Arizona valley where she was going to be tried for the murder of a man she'd never met. A man who'd died a century before she was born.

Nothing in Vera's law enforcement experience had prepared her to deal with this bizarre situation. Nothing in her personal background provided a clue she could use to discover a route back through space to her own place in time.

She laughed wryly. Too bad she hadn't paid more attention during her college physics classes. A smattering of scientific background might have provided her passport to the future.

A movement by the bed caught her attention. Jericho stood beside the tall bedstead, a heavy flannel robe dangling from his fingertips. He handed her the robe and nodded toward the mahogany washstand in the corner. "I brought you a kettle of hot water for washing up. Cook sent up some fresh rolls and butter. Better hurry before they get cold.''

She nodded. Since the interruption of their short interlude of near intimacy, Jericho was taking great pains to keep all contact detached, impersonal. What emotional tempest hid behind those dark eyes? What secrets did he cover with that outthrust jaw, so firmly constructed it might have been carved out of ironwood?

She needed to put this...infatuation with Jericho Jackson into perspective. He was like a lovely, dark-eyed puppy gazing adoringly from a pet store window. Vera could admire him, but she couldn't have him. Not for her own. She had no time for a puppy or a relationship. Her lease wouldn't allow a dog, and the century separating her and Jackson wouldn't allow a relationship. *Smile at the sweet puppy and go on your way.*

Forcing her mouth to curve upward in an impersonal smile, she looked up, avoiding his eyes. ''Thanks, I'll be right out.''

''Vera, I, uh, this is going to be all right, you know.''

She tucked her arm in the sleeve of the heavy bathrobe. Pretending total fascination with the process of donning the garment, she murmured, ''Of course it will. No sweat.''

''Pardon?''

''Nothing. Just an expression.'' A dry laugh escaped her lips. They didn't even speak the same language. She had an insane urge to pepper him with the slang, gangsta rap and buzzwords that had replaced conversation in civilized society. *Yo, Jer. Let's have a hands-on interface and brainstorm a game plan. Maybe we can find a loose circuit in the hard drive and downsize ourselves out of this virtual reality dreamscape.*

He couldn't possibly grasp the world that molded her thoughts, words and personality. What could she tell Jericho of the twentieth century? A man from these rich and unfettered times would collapse in dismayed shock to learn about congested freeways, governmental licenses required for everything from marriage to dog tags, skyrocketing taxes, intrusive telephones, E-mail, fax machines, free sex and AIDS. What would he think of an entire culture governed by sporting events and MTV?

Maybe he'd think that living in the past wasn't so bad. In a way, Vera would be sorry to leave this simpler era.

She sensed Jericho watching her, that wary, quizzical expression on his face. Obviously, he thought she'd drifted into madness again. Finally, he turned away. "I'll wait for you in the other room."

A second later, his warm and bolstering presence was gone.

DEPUTY HAMBLIN HAD EATEN at least half of the yeasty breakfast rolls by the time Vera emerged from the bedroom. With her blue-black hair pulled into a twist at the back of her head, her gaunt face stood out in pale relief.

Jericho's heart lurched at the difference in her appearance and demeanor since he'd hauled her out of the mine shaft. Those blue smudges under her eyes hadn't been there before. He was certain. She looked thinner. The hollows beneath her cheekbones more pronounced.

And she looked infinitely sadder. The struggle to clear her name had stolen all her spit and fire. Her shoulders sagged and she kept chewing on her lower lip, as if the uncertainty of her life expectancy could no longer be endured.

Although he knew it was crazy, Jericho felt somehow responsible for the changes he saw. As if by failing to help her resolve Rafe's murder, he'd personally condemned her to the gallows.

Guilt slashed his belly. Hadn't he done just that by doing nothing?

Sure, he'd taken her in and hidden her. Even given her money, though God alone knew what she'd done with it while she was in that…vague state. But Vera was the only one who'd actively tried to uncover the real murderer. She'd gone against her own nature and donned dance hall finery, sang slightly bawdy songs before a teeming mass of woman-hungry males and chatted and joked with these men. All for the purpose of finding someone, anyone, who might have a fragment of information about Rafe Wilson's death.

And what had fine, upstanding citizen Jackson done to aid in her pursuit of the truth? Not a damned thing.

As she moved easily into the room, dressed now in those denim trousers she was wearing that first day, he watched with awed admiration as she threw her shoulders back and gave Deputy Hamblin a weak smile. Why hadn't Jericho raised a finger to help her?

The truth washed over him like the icy melt-off at the first thaw. Because in his gut, hidden away where he couldn't examine his reasons too closely, he guarded the secret knowledge that if Vera's name was cleared and she was given her freedom, she'd leave him and never return.

And he selfishly wanted her to stay. He liked hearing her hoots of laughter, liked seeing the unstudied light in her eyes when she encountered something she'd never seen before.

Like a child who hides beneath the bed, believing if he can't see the goblin it can't get him, Jericho had hidden from the truth. He'd never really believed the law would arrest her. Thought somehow he could keep her, a singing bird in his own golden cage, until…until what?

He didn't know. Just didn't know.

Balancing a porcelain cup of steaming coffee, Vera walked over to stand in front of him. Only the faint tremble of her bottom lip gave away the raw emotion she was trying so valiantly to hide. "Mr. Hamblin says the railroad isn't functioning so we're going down the mountain by mule."

Jericho nodded. The narrow gauge railroad was often closed down during winter months. Keeping the tracks cleared of snow was nearly impossible given the rugged terrain. During the best of times, the incline was so steep, so twisting, that the locomotive could only sustain five cars.

The hairpin turns were so sharp in some places, rumor had it the passengers liked to hang their heads out the windows to get a look at their rear ends.

He nodded. At this time of year, descent into the Chino Valley and Prescott was best accomplished by pack mules. "Henry's right. It's safest to travel by mule."

She glanced over her shoulder where the deputy was stuffing another buttered roll into his mouth. "Mr. Hamblin had a quaint way of phrasing it. He said some trails are only 'jackassable.'"

Jericho chuckled. "That's one way of putting it. Still, if the weather holds, you should make the valley floor sometime tomorrow."

Vera's head jerked up. "Aren't...aren't you coming with us?"

Jericho shook his head. Until five minutes ago, he'd planned on doing exactly that. Now, he thought he'd hang behind. Make sure no one followed them down the mountain and, maybe, pick up a shred of unguarded conversation. If the real killer thought he'd gotten away with murder, he might loosen up a bit. Might say or do something to give himself away if someone was paying close attention.

While Jericho knew that Vera needed his moral support, she needed his help more. He hoped someday she would understand why he appeared to be abandoning her now. Not wanting her to raise her expectations beyond his abilities, he decided to keep his plans to himself for the moment. "I've got some things to attend to here in town. I'll see you in Prescott."

"If I'm still alive," she said archly. Her cup and saucer clattered onto the mahogany side table.

Jericho knew she was disappointed in him, but he didn't know how to reassure her, so he said nothing.

She straightened her shoulders and pointedly turned toward Henry Hamblin. "Might as well get this show on the road, Deputy. Are you ready?"

"Mmmf," he mumbled, stuffing the last morsel of roll into his mouth and grabbing his hat.

Vera slung her knapsack over her shoulder. "Ready when you are."

Hamblin reached for her backpack. "I'll need to search that, Miz McBride."

She raised an eyebrow. "I don't have a gun if that's what you're thinking."

"No ma'am, I doubt you do. Still, rules say I have to check for myself."

Vera surrendered the rucksack.

The deputy opened the nylon fastener and peered inside. He scratched his head and dumped the contents out onto the settee. One by one, he picked up her personal items and shoved them back inside: comb, hairbrush, change purse, and hand lotion. A few things he kept out.

"What's this stuff?" Hamblin poked at several items he obviously couldn't identify.

Jericho watched the color rise in Vera's cheeks as she snatched up a paper-wrapped tube of some kind and stuffed it back inside the canvas pouch. "It's personal female stuff," she snapped. "The kind of things men shouldn't ask about unless they're ready to be embarrassed."

"Oh."

Jericho covered his mouth so Hamblin wouldn't

see him grin. Even though most of the men in town stepped aside when Henry Hamblin loped down the sidewalk, he made it a rule never to argue with his wife. Matilda Hamblin was a formidable woman and Henry had long learned to accommodate her. It was obvious the lawman had developed a wary respect for female matters.

Vera picked up a couple of odd-looking containers. She flipped a cap off one and pressed a button on the top. A soft, flowery aroma filled the air. "This is cologne."

"Never seen it squirt out like that before," Hamblin exclaimed.

Jericho's eyes rolled. "How long since you bought Matilda an atomizer of fragrance, Hamblin? You ought to be ashamed."

Grabbing the containers from Vera's hands, the deputy shoved all her belongings back inside the canvas bag. "Buying women's fripperies ain't to my liking, Jackson. Not ever'one's a ladies' man like you."

Hoisting the straps of the bag over her shoulder, Vera stepped between them. "I hate to interrupt this session of the ole boys club, but hadn't we better get moving? The sooner we get to Prescott the sooner I can clear my name."

The slight note of levity dissolved, as if someone had poured hot water onto a lump of sugar.

Stepping forward, Jericho reached for Vera's shoulders, but she backed away from his grasp. Stretching out her arm, she offered her hand. "I want to thank you for all your hospitality, Jericho. It meant the world to me."

"Maybe I should explain why I'm not going—"

"No!" She held up her hand, stopping his explanation. "It's…it's not necessary. You've done far more than I, uh, a near-stranger could ever expect. You've ignored your business far too long already on my behalf. I just wanted you to know I appreciated your taking me in."

A near-stranger? Ignoring his business? Were her feelings for him so shallow that they couldn't survive one perceived failure on his part? How could she have fallen into his arms with such abandon last night, to treat him like a mere acquaintance this morning? He realized he'd disappointed her, but she should have more faith in him than to think this damned saloon meant more to him than her life.

Even if they'd never moved beyond the friendship stage, his debt to her mother and basic human decency would have demanded he do everything in his power to help her. For Vera to imply that he'd forsaken her because of business cut into him like a rusty sword. She'd inflicted a wound that would take a very long time to heal.

Unable to speak, he simply nodded and walked to the door. Holding it open while Deputy Hamblin escorted her into the dimly lit hallway, Jericho watched in silence until they descended the staircase and disappeared from sight.

His hurt building to an anger that bordered on rage, he stalked back inside and slammed the door.

FOUR HOURS LATER Vera was so saddle sore she felt like her backside must have swollen to twice its normal size. When Deputy Hamblin held up his hand to signal a rest stop, she could have kissed him.

Easing off the jenny, whom the deputy had obtained for her use, Vera rubbed her aching fanny and walked around the small clearing. If she lived long enough to get down this mountain, she vowed never again to climb onto the back of any animal. Especially one that moved with the rolling, jostling, jarring gait reminiscent of a drunken sailor.

After tying their mounts to a tree limb and giving them water, Hamblin ambled over to where Vera was still massaging her backside. "Uh, if you need to take a trip into the bushes, I'll unroll a saddle blanket to give you some privacy."

That took her attention off her throbbing posterior. "If I go back into the bushes far enough, you won't need to do that."

Hamblin took off his hat and rolled it around his fingertips in a nervous gesture. "No ma'am, I can't rightly let you out of my sight until I turn you over to the sheriff in Prescott."

Vera's arms flew outward, encompassing the endless wilderness. "Come on, Deputy, look around you. We're a hundred miles from civilization and you have the mules right here beside you. Where do you expect me to go?"

He shook his head doubtfully. "Iffen it was any other lady but you, Miz McBride, I could take your point. But ever'body knows you can find your way around this mountain like a mother bear finding her squawling cubs. No, ma'am, if I let you go off alone, you'd be smokin' a peace pipe with your kin before I even knew you was gone."

"That's ridiculous. Then I'll just forgo the pleasure for a while longer." She flopped to the ground, cringing when her tender bottom made contact with the still-frozen ground.

Hamblin reached into his hip pocket and pulled out a set of crude-looking handcuffs. "Well, it's your choice, Miz McBride, but I'm afraid I can't hold my water as well as you. So you just make yourself comfortable right here until I get back."

Too tired to protest, she held out her arms. Having the decency to look chagrined, the deputy snapped the heavy cuffs around her wrists, then ratcheted them until they fit snugly. "Make sure they're tight enough. I wouldn't want you to take any chances that a dangerous, notorious criminal could flee justice while in your custody."

Vera knew her words were heavy with sarcasm and that she was taking her frustration out on the hapless lawman. But she was exhausted and frightened. And wished Jericho was here.

When Hamblin wandered into a stand of head-high mesquite bushes, she allowed her mind to roam over the satirical aspects of the past few days. That she, a peace officer, was now a shackled prisoner accounted for only the most blatant irony. She'd come to Arizona in the first place to find out what had become of her long-lost ancestor, Verity McBride. She was about to discover the girl's grisly fate from a firsthand perspective.

Perhaps the most ironic aspect of this entire, unreal

episode was her unexpected...appreciation for Jericho Jackson. Oh, the man's frontier chauvinism occasionally drove her wild. Nor did she understand what motivated and drove him. Yet, she'd never imagined she'd find a man she felt so comfortable with, a man she could rely on, a man who rang her chimes until her toenails tickled.

Yet she'd found all these things in Jericho.

Sadly, he was lost to her from the moment they'd met. Not only were they divided by opposing cultures, goals and societies, but by a broken fragment of time that separated their destinies by more than a hundred years.

He, too, must have sensed the futility of their budding relationship. How else could she explain his sudden coldness this morning? His bland statement that he was going to remain behind?

She'd never forget how abandoned and utterly alone she'd felt when he said he wasn't accompanying her to Prescott. It was as if she'd lost friend, lover and mentor all in a single moment. Even now, the empty feeling in her stomach made her feel like a fish who'd been jerked from its supply of life-sustaining water, then gutted and filleted.

Her body was only an empty shell. Her heart, soul and the vibrant parts that comprised Vera McBride had somehow turned to dust.

She wondered if she'd ever see Jericho again.

A harsh, stinging lump formed in her throat and she swallowed deeply to stave off the hot tears behind her eyes. She wouldn't cry over this man. She wouldn't.

A rustling sound in the bushes behind her told her that Deputy Hamblin had completed his nature call. As he stepped back into the clearing and sauntered toward his mule, he grinned. "Whew, feel much better. Forgot to ask if you wanted a drink of water." He unlooped a canteen strap from his saddle pommel.

He started unscrewing the cap as he walked toward her. "Sure you don't want to change your mind about—"

The earsplitting sound of a rifle blast cut off the rest of his words.

Chapter Twelve

A shrill scream reverberated in the air just after the gunshot.

With a jolt of surprise, Vera realized the scream had issued from her own lips.

Henry Hamblin stared at her. His eyes widened in disbelief. The canteen fell slowly from his fingers and clattered on the hard ground. Vera watched in horror as a bright red stain blossomed across the front of his shirt, beneath his open sheepskin jacket.

Looking like a character in a western movie, the deputy clutched his chest and fell forward slowly and dramatically, as if drawing out his last scene in hopes of an Oscar nomination.

He sagged onto his knees for a heart-rending moment before falling facedown in the dirt across Vera's legs. He didn't cry out with pain or protest. A soft gurgling from somewhere deep in his chest was the only sound in the too still air.

Vera's heart thundered out a fierce, erratic rhythm. She lowered her manacled hands to his head as she numbly searched for a pulse point in his neck. "Deputy Hamblin? Henry? Oh sweet heaven, are you all right?''

But she knew the answer to that inane question. She'd seen fatal gunshot wounds often enough to recognize the death rattle emanating from his throat. Henry Hamblin was at death's door and there was nothing she could do to help him.

A violent tremble took hold of his body and Vera leaned over, lending her heat to his. For the briefest second she felt his fingers clutch convulsively at her leg, then, his grip loosened and a small shudder rippled through his large body.

The gurgling sound ceased. The good-natured lawman was dead.

Vera didn't know how long she sat there, bent over the deputy's lifeless body. Her mind was blank, her body numb. She wasn't aware of the cold, her hunger or her fear.

She had no doubt she'd been spared death yet again. The killer surely had been aiming for her when he'd accidentally struck Deputy Hamblin. The fact that the lawman was still ten feet away from her when the bullet struck him was of no consequence. She knew these ancient firearms were notorious for their inaccuracy.

It was only a matter of moments now until the murderer came in closer for the kill. Next time he wouldn't miss and Vera was too mentally and physically exhausted to care. At least it would all be over soon.

As the dead man's blood cooled on her legs, Vera

leaned back against the trunk of a scrub oak, closed her eyes, and waited for her executioner.

She'd almost drifted into a listless sleep when she heard the thrumming beat of approaching hooves. Now, she thought, would be a good time to talk to her maker. Maybe a last-minute plea for mercy.

Apparently the rider was taking no chances on missing his target again for he galloped directly into the clearing. She could hear the horse snorting from exertion. Although she'd accepted her imminent death, a sliver of curiosity poked at her. If she was going to die, at least she ought to know who was taking her life. A last wish for the condemned; see the real murderer. Her cuffed hands still resting on Hamblin's neck, she raised her head and opened her eyes.

Jericho was striding toward her, his black eyes flashing with high emotion.

Instinctively, she sucked in a deep breath as the truth struck her like a heavy rock hurled into her stomach. Jericho was the sniper.

The final irony broke her heart. Her first instinct about Jericho had been right all along. She remembered that first ride into Jerome when he'd insisted on hiding from the posse. She'd thought then that he was a killer. Now it seemed her suspicions were validated.

"Vera! My God! Are you all right?" Dropping to his knees beside her, Jericho slipped his hands beneath Hamblin's lifeless body and gently flipped him onto his back. Her legs tingled when the heavy weight was removed.

Jericho threw aside his black hat and lowered his head onto the deputy's bloodied chest. He listened in silence and shook his head. "He's gone," Jericho whispered unnecessarily. "We've got to get you out of here."

He scrambled to his feet and reached down for her hand, pulling her to her feet. Spying the silver cuffs at her wrist, he bent over and fumbled through Hamblin's pockets until he extracted the key. With a deft flick of his wrist, Jericho opened the cuffs, freeing her hands.

"Thank you," she murmured, wondering what she was supposed to be feeling. Outrage? Disgust? She only felt terribly sad.

It all made sense. A terrible, horrific logical sense.

Jericho must have been Rafe's business partner. Hadn't she known all along that Rafe Wilson had no money? Of course he'd seek out a partner who could capitalize his venture—whatever it was. Something to do with mining, no doubt.

There must have been a falling out of thieves. Jericho was a friend and frequent visitor to Verity's home. He must have happened along right after she assaulted her stepfather and fled into the night.

Quick to see the advantage, Jericho decided to eliminate his partner and keep the proceeds of their enterprise for himself. Why share a tasty pie when he could have the whole thing for himself? Vera knew there were no contracts, no papers tying partnerships into neat little bundles in the Old West.

How Jericho must have laughed to himself when

Verity turned to him for help. Talk about the poor little fly stepping into the tarantula's web.

Glancing around the clearing, Jericho hurried her across the clearing and helped her mount the jenny. How could she have been so dreadfully wrong? She'd cared for...maybe even loved this man. Obviously he'd decided he couldn't allow her to stand trial for fear his own guilt would be exposed.

But now that he'd killed the lawman by mistake, what were his plans for Vera?

She had to find out, had to pretend she still believed in his innocence, had to fool him into a false sense of security in order to get him to reveal his intentions. As her aching backside once more adjusted to the saddle, she asked, "What about the deputy? We can't just leave him lying there."

After securing Henry's mount to his saddle with a sturdy rope, Jericho slipped his foot into the stirrup and climbed aboard his horse. "We don't have a choice. When we get to Prescott I'll send someone to recover his body. We're like sitting ducks as long as we stay here. We have to keep moving."

She nodded mutely. Taking the reins of her jackass, he clucked his tongue, and they started back down the steep trail. Keep him talking, she thought. Keep him ignorant as to the extent of her knowledge. Vera repeated these words over and over to herself as they picked their way down the rock-strewn path. The only weapons she had were her wits and the shreds of her courage, and Vera instinctively knew she'd need them both before this day was over.

They only stopped for rest once during that interminable ride. Judging from the position of the sun, Vera guessed it was midafternoon when Jericho finally drew up near a shallow stream.

"The animals are tired," he said. "If we don't give them a rest we might find ourselves on foot. We should be safe enough here. At least for a while."

He pointed to a sharp promontory jutting out from the side of the cactus-littered mountainside. "That rock formation will keep us hidden from the view of our friend up there."

Her gaze followed his pointing finger. He was hinting that someone else, not him, was the sniper. Oh, how she wished she could believe him. But who else had the motive and opportunity? None of her talks with men at the saloon had uncovered information. Who else knew she was alone on this particular miserable trail with Deputy Hamblin?

No, maybe Jericho was playing mind games. Trying to keep her off stride until he could decide what to do. Since they'd left the clearing, Vera had done nothing more than think about why Jericho hadn't gone ahead and finished her off when he'd killed Deputy Hamblin.

She'd figured it out only a few minutes before. When the deputy's body was found, it wouldn't take a modern autopsy to determine he'd been killed by a rifle from a long distance. Did Jericho plan to pin this second killing on her as well? She might have been able to explain away one death, but two?

She had little doubt that somewhere farther along the trail Jericho would pull his gun and shoot her dead. Then, he could haul her body into Prescott and announce he'd slain a wanted fugitive. Once word got around that she'd also murdered the well-liked Henry Hamblin, Jericho would be hailed as a hero.

It was hard—nearly impossible—to believe this of a man who'd kissed her so passionately...but what if it were true? Vera's life was at stake here—and she had no choice but to assume the worst. Otherwise, the only chance she had was to stay alert and somehow outmaneuver Jericho.

After tethering their mounts to a lacy paloverde tree, he unsheathed his heavy bowie knife and chipped away at the thin covering of ice that coated the nearby stream. Immediately, the mules lowered their lathered necks and sipped at the refreshing water.

Stepping around to her side, Jericho reached up to help her dismount. "You're awfully quiet."

As soon as her toes touched ground, she pulled away from his touch. Her traitorous senses couldn't grasp that he was possibly a cold-blooded killer. She still tingled like a tuning fork whenever he touched her. And she hated the weakness, the debilitating loneliness that made her still want him. She reminded herself she had to be careful. In response to his question, she crossed her arms over her chest. "I guess having a decent man murdered at my feet kind of quells any urge for casual conversation."

Jericho's expressive black eyebrow soared. "You're still angry because I didn't come with you this morning," he accused.

"No, trust me, I'm not."

After they rested Jericho handed her a small bundle

wrapped with a calico neckerchief. "What's this?" she said.

"Food. Got to keep up your strength but you'll have to eat while we ride. I don't want to give our friend too much time to sneak up on us."

She nodded mutely. Holding the bundle between her clenched teeth, she wrapped both hands around the pommel and stepped into Jericho's interlaced fingers. Using every last weary fiber of her strength, she hoisted herself back into the saddle.

Once again they set off down the steep mountain trail. She could only hope her suspicions about Jericho were unfounded. But if they were, that also meant a killer was following them.

THE SUN WAS GOING DOWN behind the mountains. Royal purple and soft pink streaks painted the western sky in the vivid manner of a Gauguin landscape. The first star twinkled dimly on the horizon.

Vera had passed weary, gone beyond exhaustion and felt she was near an unconscious stupor when Jericho finally turned around in his saddle. "Guess we can hole up over there for the night."

He pointed to a tiny tuck in the mountainside. "We'll be protected on three sides."

"What about—him?" Vera hitched a thumb up the trail behind them, still hoping she was wrong to fear Jericho—and yet terrified because someone was responsible for the two deaths.

Jericho dismounted and came alongside to help Vera down. "Only a fool would venture down that narrow trail in the dark. Besides, if he's riding a jackass like most folks do in these parts, it'll stop dead when it can't see any longer. I reckon we're safe enough 'til morning.''

They led the animals to a protected clearing hidden from view by a stand of huge granite boulders. The same streambed flowed nearby. Because they were now at a much lower elevation, no covering of ice hid the crystal clear water. The animals ambled over and drank greedily.

When they'd all had their fill of the refreshing water, she helped unsaddle them. Then Jericho scattered some grain onto the ground. ''Good job, ladies,'' he murmured, scratching his horse's ear. She nickered softly in reply and went back to her search for the grain. ''You deserve a treat.'' He gave Vera's jenny a good-natured smack on her sturdy rump.

Vera bit her lip and turned away. How could a man so soft, so tender to animals be a cold-blooded killer? It didn't make sense. Surely she'd leapt to the wrong conclusion when Jericho had ridden into camp earlier? Oh, how badly she wanted to believe that. But she couldn't take anything at face value. Her eyes darted around. Escape was impossible. She'd never make it on her own out here.

They hauled their bedrolls and saddlebags back to the sheltered clearing and wordlessly laid them out side by side. The icy night wind was only somewhat banished by the three-sided shelter. Vera shivered and pulled her coat closer.

He handed her both nearly empty canteens. ''If you'll fetch some water from the stream, I'll see about building us a little fire. I don't know about you but I could use a little warmth and a lot of coffee right about now."

She glanced sharply at the mountain trail, now barely visible in the heavy dusk. "A fire? Won't that be like a beacon to the sniper?"

Despite herself, she found herself half believing that someone was above them on the trail. Stalking their every move.

Jericho's gaze followed hers and he shrugged. "I'll keep it small but we need the heat. My guess is he's already settled down for the night, hoping to get the jump on us when daylight comes. And, like I said, only a fool would follow the Last Ride Road after dark."

Vera grimaced. They sure had a lot of colorful, if morbid, names in these parts. Dead Man's Trail, Last Ride Road. She'd grown up watching old Roy Rogers reruns where they'd closed the show singing "Happy Trails to You." Given a choice, she preferred Roy and Dale's take on the Old West over reality.

Taking the canteens from Jericho's outstretched hand, she ambled back toward the small creek. His horse and the pair of mules were munching peacefully on a few mounds of sagebrush that had survived the cold weather. It was a peaceful almost idyllic evening and yet a cold chill of apprehension rippled through her as she dropped to her knees beside the streambed and held the first canteen under the icy water. When it filled, she screwed on the cap and dipped the second one.

Suddenly, she became aware of an unnatural quiet. Tilting her head, she glanced behind her. The animals stood with their ears pricked, their nostrils flared. Suddenly, Jericho's horse started pawing at the ground.

"What's wrong, girl?" Vera whispered.

The jenny snorted and bucked, trying to escape her tethered reins. Hastily recapping the second canteen, Vera rose to her feet. She stepped toward the frightened animals, wondering if a snake had spooked them.

She wished she had heavy boots like Jericho's instead of her Nikes. Holding the canteen straps tightly in her left hand, Vera cautiously scanned the ground. Didn't rattlers go away in cold weather?

Jericho's horse whinnied loudly and reared up onto her hind legs. Her flashing hooves almost struck Vera's temple, and she backed quickly away from the frightened beast. "Easy, girl, easy. What is it?"

Then she heard it.

A low, snarling growl that caused the flesh to rise on her arms. Vera whirled around.

A large golden cat, maybe five feet from head to the tip of its twitching tail, was perched on a stand of boulders not ten feet away. Its mouth was open, exposing inch-long fangs.

"Grrreah." The mountain lion growled again and raised up on its haunches.

Although she'd never before seen a creature like this in its natural habitat, Vera knew beyond a doubt it was readying itself to strike. And she was its helpless prey.

JERICHO LEANED BACK against the hardscrabble mountain slope and admired the small fire. It had been so long since he'd eaten dust on a trail ride that he'd gotten soft. A few years ago he'd thought nothing of curling into his blanket roll and snoozing through the long frosty nights.

This fire would be a magnet if the bushwhacker was still following closely behind. Although Jericho hadn't mentioned it to Vera, he'd kept a close eye on the trail behind them. Once or twice he'd glimpsed a dust cloud, like one a horse kicked up when it was being ridden hard.

He hoped the killer would bide his time, knowing Jericho was aware of his presence. A patient man would wait until they were in a more vulnerable spot where he could easily pick them both off. At least, that's how Jericho had justified building a campfire.

He cocked his head, listening to the still night. The killer could be six feet away for all he could see in the deepening dusk. Still, the fire would warm Vera and that was reason enough to take the risk.

While he waited for her to return with the coffee water, he unholstered his sidearm and double-checked that it was fully loaded. He couldn't be too prepared not with Vera's life on the line.

Thinking of Vera caused him to wonder what was taking her so long. He raised his head and squinted into the near darkness in the direction she'd taken. Couldn't take that long to fill a couple of canteens.

He frowned, wondering if he should go check on her.

Opening the burlap sack of coffee, he measured the grounds into the coffeepot. What if something had happened to her?

There'd been no gunshot, and it was unlikely the bushwhacker could pass by their shelter without making enough noise for Jericho to notice. Still, she'd been gone a while.

He stood up and took a couple tentative steps toward the creek. Maybe he should wait a few more minutes. He'd hate to go barging up if she was…tending to personal business.

Wracked with indecision, Jericho scratched his head and busied himself pulling out their food supplies in preparation for fixing their dinner. He hunkered down and cut a chunk of fat off a thick slab of beefsteak. Using it like butter, he seasoned the cast iron skillet.

He reached for the sack of cornmeal, but realized he couldn't even mix the batter until she returned with the drinking water.

Wiping his hands on the seat of his black trousers, he strode a few feet toward the streambed. "Vera? Everything all right?"

The whispery evening wind picked up his voice and misted it across the open clearing. She didn't answer; all he could hear was the agitated shuffling of their animals. His horse whinnied, a sharp cry of fear. Something—or someone—had spooked her bad. Why hadn't Vera called for him?

Jericho dropped the sack of cornmeal and sprinted toward the creek, drawing his Colt as he ran. "Vera!"

He rounded the tall outcrop of granite boulders and spied Vera standing stock-still a few feet from Buckshot. Even in the near darkness, he could see the whites of her eyes, widened in stark terror.

Swinging his gun arm around the clearing, he stopped dead when he spotted the mountain lion.

"Grrrowww!" The enraged feline snarled at the new interloper. Its golden haunches inched higher and Jericho knew it was ready to pounce. Vera stood directly below the provoked creature, within easy striking range of its slashing claws and ripping incisors.

His heart in his throat, Jericho raised the revolver and fired three quick bursts into the night sky.

The powerful cat jolted onto its pads and bolted away from the clearing, disappearing into a crevice between a pair of huge granite rocks.

If Jericho had been ten seconds later he might have been too late to save Vera's life. The realization zapped the strength from his muscles and he sank to the ground in a spent heap.

After a moment the quaking stopped and he rose unsteadily to his feet. Taking the two short steps to her side, he wrapped both arms around her slender shoulders and held on for dear life. "Keeping you alive is turning into a full-time occupation," he whispered against the sweet flesh of her cheek.

She sagged against him, her hand patting his shoulder and upper back as if confirming for herself that he was all in one piece. "I thought you were a goner," she murmured. "And you saved my life."

He pulled back and laughed. Holding her precious face between his palms, he slowly shook his head. "Of course I saved you. Did you really think I'd let a mountain lion have you, sugar? And nothing's going to happen to me. But if you don't stop aggravating the local wildlife, I'm not too sure you're going to end the week in a single piece.''

She laughed, even though his words were too close to the terrible truth to be funny. Jericho knew her laughter was a release of tension, letting go of the fear for a few short minutes.

Anxious to keep the mood lighthearted, he glanced at the canteens dangling from her fingers. ''I suppose you spilled the water?''

Raising the heavy jugs to eye level, she grinned. ''No way. I didn't lose a drop.''

He took them from her grasp and draped an arm around her waist. ''Then let's see about fixing some grub. A man's got to keep his strength up if he's going to consort with you.''

''Consort? Doesn't that mean to, uh, cohabitate, or, um—?''

He pulled her closer. ''That's exactly what it means,'' he confirmed.

Vera didn't say another word until they reached the camp. The small fire was burning low so he added a few more mesquite branches and poured half a canteen of water into the coffeepot and set it on the flames.

A half hour later, the corn bread had baked to a golden brown and the delicious aroma of fresh coffee filled the air. Jericho turned the corn bread onto a vivid blue bandanna and threw the beefsteak into the iron skillet. He leaned back and watched the hot meat sizzle in the pan.

Vera came up beside him and lowered onto her haunches. "Mmm. Smells good."

He nodded. "Right now I'm so hungry I'd eat a rock if you'd guarantee there wasn't a snake under it."

Her fingers touched his shoulder, singeing his skin as if she'd touched him with one of the glowing embers. He glanced up to find her watching him intently, her expression wary and unreadable.

"That's three," she said softly.

"Three what?"

"Three times you've saved my life."

"Then I'd recommend you might want to keep me around."

She laughed. Her voice sounded oddly mixed with relief. "Yeah, I imagine a man like you could come in handy."

Poking a fork into the steak, he pretended to be engrossed in checking the meat. The small gesture was the only thing that prevented him from throwing her onto his saddle roll and proving to her just how "handy" he could be.

"Whew, that fire's hot. Never thought I'd say that as cold as I was a few minutes ago," she said in an abrupt shift of subject. She stepped back and lowered to the ground to sit Indian fashion, slightly behind him. "Can I ask a question?" Her voice held a wary, vigilant tone, as though she were uncertain she truly wanted an answer.

"Be my guest," he said easily.

"You've saved my life three times, yet... I—it looked like you killed Deputy Hamblin."

Jericho was so stunned he dropped the fork into the hot skillet. Slowly twisting his head, he gazed at her face, lit with shadows and highlights from the flickering orange fire. He'd never seen a woman so lovely, or so damnably infuriating.

Struggling to keep his voice level and nonthreatening, he asked, "Now why in the name of all that's sacred would you say something like that?"

She slapped her palm on her thighs, the stinging sound reverberating in the sudden quiet. "How else do you explain happening onto the scene, miles from town, just seconds after the deputy was killed? And don't tell me it was a coincidence because I don't believe in coincidences."

He stared at her for a long time, trying to digest the peculiar set of beliefs that governed this enigmatic woman. He couldn't believe this was the same unsophisticated female he'd known most of her life. It was as if she'd flown down from the moon or something.

"You've known me for how many years? A lot, anyway. Yet you can sit here and tell me that you honestly believe that I murdered one of my best friends in cold blood?"

Vera's head ducked and she stared at her fingers that were interlaced in her lap. "Put like that it doesn't sound very likely."

"It isn't very damned likely no matter how you word it! Damn, now the meat's burning!"

He turned around and grabbed the fork handle to turn the meat. "Ouch!" he dropped it again. The fool thing was almost white-hot.

Rising to her knees, Vera crawled up beside him. "Let me see."

She took his hand in hers and examined the burned skin, already beginning to blister. "I don't suppose you brought any eggs with you?"

"Yeah, there's three or four in that pouch, but you should put butter or lard on the burn."

Vera reached for the saddlebag he'd pointed to and extracted an egg. Reaching for one of the tin cups he'd set out for their coffee, she broke the egg white into the cup, saving the yolk in the eggshell. "Here, smear this on your hand, it'll stop the sting right away. Lard would only deep fry it."

He started to protest but stopped. Her mother, Mine-wah, was known throughout the territory as a healer. This must be one of her folk remedies, he decided. The soothing egg white took out the sting in a matter of seconds and Jericho looked at her in awed surprise. "Your mother is a genius."

"I beg your pardon?"

"This is working better than a dollar potion from a medicine show."

"I'll take that as a compliment. But the steak is still burning." Pushing him aside, she picked up the other fork and deftly turned the meat.

Nothing more was mentioned about her suspicions while they finished preparing their simple meal. After they'd eaten their fill and leaned back, replete, to watch the starscape in the midnight blue sky, Jericho turned and took her chin between his fingers.

"Let's get this hashed out once and for all. I did not kill Rafe Wilson or Henry Hamblin. Furthermore, my intentions toward you damn sure aren't honorable but they aren't lethal, either.''

She started to reply but his fingertips inched upward, stilling her lips. ''Let me finish. I didn't just happen on you on the trail. I deliberately lagged behind hoping one of the men would loosen up a bit once you were out of the way. Jess Wiggins is so ticked at me he says he isn't even *drinking* in the Copper Penny anymore, much less talking to the likes of me.

''So, when it became clear there wasn't any new gossip that could help your cause, I set out to catch up with you. I...I didn't want you facing the folks in Prescott on your own.''

''Oh, Jericho, I—''

''Shhh. I'm almost finished. You see, I truly don't understand what's going on. You seem so...so different somehow. But one thing's clear as sunlight to me, and that's that you didn't shoot Rafe Wilson in the back. And they'll string me up first before I let anybody lay a hand on you.''

That was the biggest speech he'd ever made in his life and Jericho was emotionally drained. He blew out a deep breath and waited for her reaction which was swift and totally unexpected.

Huge wet tears filled her warm brown eyes and she threw her arms around his neck. ''Oh, Jericho, I've been such a fool. I've just been so frustrated and confused. And when the attempts started on my life I just...just stop thinking straight, I guess.''

''Hush now. We don't need to speak of it again.''

He reached up and dabbed at the dampness under her spiky black eyelashes.

Why'd she have to go and turn on the waterworks?

Jericho leaned forward and lightly kissed the edge of her eyes, savoring the salty tears. His mouth trailed downward, to the plane of her cheek, then the tip of her nose before coming to rest, at long last, on the luscious sweetness of her mouth.

An errant tear had reached her upper lip and he delicately licked it away. She shivered with delight and opened her mouth, inviting him in.

For a mere instant Min-e-wah's accusing eyes flashed in his mind. She'd entrusted her daughter to his care. God help him, he owed Min-e-wah his life. But no man could resist the lure of Vera's soft lips. He offered a quick prayer that his friend would forgive him before once more losing himself in her daughter's embrace.

As he gazed into Vera's dark eyes, Jericho knew in that moment that he was going to make love to her and anticipation filled him, thickening his loins. He'd already had a glimpse of her long, slender legs and his trousers tightened as he imagined the dark silky treasure waiting for him at the apex of those golden thighs.

Carefully padding the back of her head with his forearm, he lowered her to the bedroll. He raised up on his elbow to look at her, to devour her with his greedy eyes. Her upthrust breasts were ripe enough to burst through the thin material of his chambray shirt that she'd borrowed. A shirt that had never looked so good on him.

He looped one leg over her, settling his knee between her thighs, gently pressing against the warm mound of her womanhood.

She moaned softly and he lazily flicked open her shirt buttons, one by one, savoring and licking the tender flesh each opening exposed for his pleasure.

Never in his life had Jericho felt this incredible rush of desire for a woman. This overwhelming need to make her his own, to deeply fill her, to take her to heights of rapture she'd never imagined.

Her pleasure was all that mattered. His could wait.

When her breasts were at last unfettered, he lowered his mouth to her nipples, sucking and nuzzling each in turn until she writhed and moved beneath him, her fingers furrowing through his hair.

His tongue moved downward, teasing a trail down the tender flesh of her flat stomach until he was thwarted by the tight waistband of her denim jeans. Frustrated by the confining material, he yanked open the metal zipper and peeled the offending fabric from her legs.

She lay before him like a golden feast, only a pair of filmy drawers, the likes of which he'd never seen, barely covering her hips.

Unable to control the surge of desire that raced through him, he dropped his head and nuzzled her through the thin fabric. Her scent was rich and womanly and he ran his fingers beneath the elastic, finding at last the sweet wetness.

She raised up on her elbows, her fingers tugging at his head. "Oh, Jericho, I need you. Inside me. Now."

"No, not yet," he insisted, spreading her legs wide and moving to kneel.

With infinite slowness, he unveiled the bounty covered by the sheer fabric. He was so hard, so throbbing with need that he feared he wouldn't be able to contain himself much longer. But he had to. This was about Vera and his need to please her. His own aching desire could wait.

When his mouth moved to take her, she cried out, a wild frenzied sound that only spurred his heated desire.

Suddenly, he couldn't take the weight of his clothing pressing against his body. Reluctantly pulling his mouth from her sweetness, he sat up and yanked off his clothes until he lay naked beside her.

"My turn," she whispered, pushing his shoulders back against the hard ground.

She licked her lips and drew a bead down his body with her tongue, dissecting him into a quivering mass of need. When her mouth settled on him, he groaned once, unable to stand the skittery pleasure boiling in his loins.

Pulling her head from him, he drew her upward until she settled on him. Fitting him like a custom glove, a sweet, wet yielding glove.

For a long moment they rode the crest of desire together, then he felt her tighten around him and she cried out again with her pleasure. Jericho lost complete control when she reached her peak. With a shuddering moan, he reached his own climax and they collapsed together, totally spent.

Lazily lifting her head, she grinned. "That was

number four. You're a true lifesaver, Jericho Jackson.''

A moment later, she was asleep on top of him. Her warm breath a wreath circling his face. The scent of their togetherness a heady reminder of the stolen moments they'd shared.

A coyote howled in the distance, bringing Jericho back to the present. He was grateful for their brief respite, and still stunned by the strength and depth of their lovemaking. Unfortunately, their coming together hadn't really changed anything.

The sun would be up in a few hours, bringing back the problems that had brought them to this forsaken place in the wilderness.

Jericho blew a strand of her silky hair from his mouth. He wanted to hold her against him, protect her from the world, but he knew he couldn't.

He also knew the odds weren't very good that they'd both survive long enough to share another night.

Chapter Thirteen

The cold night wind whistling across her bare back brought Vera out of the soundest sleep she'd enjoyed in...in years. She stretched and felt Jericho's firmly muscled body move in concert with hers.

A catlike grin on her face, she slid off and nestled beside him.

"Mmm," he murmured.

"Mmm yourself. If we don't get some clothes on they'll find our frozen bodies sometime next spring," she teased.

"Our happy frozen bodies," he corrected. Opening one eye, he stared at her. "You *are* happy, aren't you?"

Vera sighed. "I suppose by happy you mean satisfied. Sexually. And yes, sated would be a better word. But as far as happiness..."

Her voice trailed off. How could she be happy, even in the arms of a man who thrilled her beyond words? She had no home, no future, no sense of the kind of life normal people took for granted. She'd hoped someday to have it all: a career, picket fence and the two-point-five children that comprised the national average.

She hadn't expected her future would find her fighting for her life in an uncivilized western society that still believed in vigilante justice.

Jericho was silent while they donned their clothing and nestled side by side. He'd added a few more twigs to the campfire and the blaze blew its comforting hot breath over them.

After a moment he said into the darkness, "All right, let's try to be logical here. We've pretty well figured out who *didn't* kill Rafe, so let's see who's most likely."

"Jess Wiggins," Vera said without thinking.

"Ole Jess is a contentious sort, no doubt about that. But he sure acts inflamed over Rafe's death."

Vera shrugged. "To cover his own guilt? He spent the most time with Rafe. They were drinking buddies. Why not business partners?"

"I don't know, maybe. But Jess Wiggins never seems to have two nickels to rub against each other. What about...Yorkie?"

"That gawky tall kid?" Vera asked in surprise.

"Yeah. He's always around, always in the background. I'm not sure he's as soft-minded as he'd like folks to think."

Vera pondered his words. "You know, you may have a point. I remember Susannah saying that Yorkie was so good at bumming drinks off everyone else that he never spent a penny. She said he probably had a bundle of greenbacks stuffed in his mattress in place of straw."

"Hmmm. Well, if anyone knows what's going on in Jerome, it's Susannah. And Stuart Greavy, of course. Folks tell the good doctor all their secrets."

Vera raised up. "Now why didn't I think of that? I should have interrogated him about Rafe's associates. The only ones I know anything about are Yorkie and Jess Wiggins. And Sally, of course."

"Sally Weaver? The blonde who deals faro at the Copper Penny? What's she got to do with Rafe?"

Vera rolled her eyes. "How can it be that men, no matter what century they're from, are all alike? I wasn't in the Copper Penny more than an hour until I'd learned she and Rafe were having an affair."

"Speaking of affairs..." Jericho rolled over and nuzzled her neck. "I know a way to keep us both warm."

Laughing slightly, Vera pushed him off. "Oh, no you don't. I just got my clothes back on."

"I can help you." He reached beneath her heavy jacket and plucked open a button.

Vera felt a responsive stirring low in her stomach, but she bit her lip and pushed his hand aside. The lovely interlude they'd shared earlier couldn't be repeated. It wasn't fair to either of them to start a relationship that didn't have a chance of success.

Jericho didn't know the truth about her; how could she explain it to him so that he wouldn't turn her back over to Doc Greavy for commitment in an asylum? Besides, she couldn't *stay* in 1896. Her home was decades forward in time. She had a job to get back to. A sick mother to tend. She owned a cat, for crying out loud!

No, Vera knew this relationship was hopeless and nothing but heartache could come of pursuing it further. Reaching out, she patted Jericho's hand. "Let's get some sleep. Tomorrow's going to come awfully early."

JERICHO DOUSED the dying embers and lightly poked Vera's leg with his boot. "Time to rise and shine, sunshine."

She raised up on her elbow and blinked. Rubbing the sleep from her eyes, she looked around the clearing. The animals were already saddled and ready to go. Jericho's bedroll was tucked neatly into place behind Buckshot's saddle.

Apparently he'd been up for some time, judging from the fragrant aroma of freshly perked coffee that wafted through the air. "It's still dark," she complained, taking the tin cup from his outstretched fingers.

"Yeah, and unless you don't care about seeing another sunrise we'd better get a move on."

Recalling the sniper that was probably only moments behind them, Vera sat up and finger-combed her hair into a knot at the back of her head. Five minutes later, they were back on the trail, nibbling cold corn bread for sustenance. The morning passed quickly. The temperature rose as they made their way to the valley floor, and when they stopped to rest, Vera shed her heavy jacket. She noted Jericho's appreciative gaze and abruptly turned away.

She had to keep focused on her goal and stop losing herself in his ink black eyes. His jaw tightened in response to her coldness and she felt a stab of shame when he retreated into that hard-edged shell of indifference he'd worn since they first met. She knew she'd hurt him, but she was powerless to change their circumstances, nor could she even explain. Jericho was a big boy and he'd get over it. She only wondered if she'd ever get over losing *him*.

"I've been thinking," he said conversationally. "I don't think we ought to turn you over to the sheriff in Prescott."

"What? You were the one who said I'd receive a fair trial and could clear my name. You said if I didn't give myself up they'd put a bounty on my head and I'd never be free. You said—"

"I was wrong." His abrupt manner took her aback. She paused, her hand on the reins and waited for him to finish.

"Henry Hamblin's death changes everything. Everybody in Jerome thinks we've been…living in sin. And, after last night, neither of us could testify that isn't so."

Baffled by how their sexual relationship entered into her murder trial, Vera sat openmouthed while he continued.

"The prosecutor's going to say that we planned this whole thing. That you shot Rafe in a squabble of some kind and then came running to me. Which you did. Then they're going to say that I followed you and Henry out of town. Which I did."

"But…"

"Yeah, but I didn't kill him. Except who's going

to believe I didn't do it to save you from a life in prison, at best?''

Vera shook her head, trying to follow his logic. ''The fact that I'm turning myself in should help prove my innocence.''

''You expect these uneducated miners to follow that serpentine logic? All they know is two men are dead, we're together and there isn't another suspect in sight. It won't take them two minutes to reach a verdict.''

The reins slipped from her fingers and Vera leaned her cheek against the jenny's scratchy hide. Jericho's awful words held the crystal clear ring of truth.

Holding up her hand, she held off further comment. Walking over to the dappled shade of an ancient paloverde, she leaned against the pale green bark. ''Let me think this through.''

''Nothing to think about,'' he said, striding over to stand in front of her. ''I'm taking you down to the Apache encampment where nobody will find you. It's the only way you'll be safe.''

''What about you?'' she countered.

''What about me?''

''You're the one who said they'd blame Deputy Hamblin's death on you. If you ride into Prescott, what's to stop them from throwing *you* in the slammer to stand trial for murder?''

''Not a damn thing,'' Jericho said in a matter-of-fact tone that told her he'd already considered and accepted that risk.

''There has to be another way,'' she insisted. ''If

only we could figure out what really happened that day.''

"How? It's not likely the killer is going to step forward and throw himself on the mercy of the court.''

"Nooo,'' she said slowly. "But maybe somebody else knows something.''

A new and frightening thought occurred to her. What if Verity had seen more than any of them suspected? That would explain why she didn't just come forward and tell her story. She had several witnesses. Her brothers and mother knew she'd only hit Rafe Wilson with a skillet before fleeing that cabin. For the umpteenth time, Vera wondered where the real Verity was....

While a jury might not believe Vera without corroboration, how could they dispute Verity's witnesses? It didn't make sense.

Maybe Verity knew something, but hadn't realized the importance of that knowledge right away. Maybe she'd later come to the realization that she could identify Rafe's killer. Wouldn't that cause her to flee? It would certainly explain why the real murderer was so anxious to silence her forever.

The real murderer had to be someone Verity believed she couldn't best in court. Someone whose word would be readily accepted over hers.

Stepping past Jericho, Vera stalked back to the jackass. The answer had to be in Verity's journal. Even though Vera had read it several times, she must have missed something. Some small clue to the killer's identity.

She slipped the journal into her blouse, hoping to read it while on the trail but the path was too twisted and strewn with rocks to make reading possible. With a sigh of disappointment, she tucked it away until they stopped for another break.

But her mind wouldn't rest. She kept replaying what she knew of the events of the past few days, hoping to pull a thread of logic from the skein of unrelated facts.

What did she know for certain? Maybe if she started with the undisputed facts she could think her way through the tangled mess.

Fact one: the killer had taken advantage of Verity's fight with her stepfather and was trying to make her a scapegoat for his crime.

Fact two: who knew about that fight? Other than Min-e-wah and the boys, only Jericho was privy to that information.

Vera sighed. At every juncture, Jericho Jackson was the cornerstone that her unsettling questions teetered upon.

When they at long last reached the valley floor, Jericho drew them to a halt. "Let's rest here and decide what to do next. Once we head out across that flat ground, we'll be sitting ducks."

More than eager to dismount and give her screaming muscles a break, she poured water into tin pie plates for the animals and carried the journal to a shaded spot that was still covered by sparse brown grass.

Sitting down, she doused her neckerchief in a bit of lukewarm water from her canteen and swabbed the sweat from her face. It was amazing how it could go from bitter cold to sweltering in a few short hours.

After slaking her thirst with the tepid water, she opened Verity's journal and read for the umpteenth time the events surrounding Rafe Wilson's death.

She read again about the terror that ruled the Wilson household, everyone holding their breath in case the abusive man came home drunk again. Then Verity wrote about her flight. The cold. The snow. Holding up in the line shack. Nothing that offered a clue to help clear her name.

Frustrated but not ready to give up, Vera skipped back a few pages and read over the notations of the weeks prior to Rafe's death. A few weeks before, Verity mentioned going into town with her stepfather for supplies. She wrote about meeting him after she'd loaded the wagon outside the assayer's office.

Had Rafe and his partner found another vein of copper?

Vera knew that during the copper mining boom, such a discovery was worth untold wealth. She recalled reading that during the late 1800s, William Clark, the owner of the United Verde Mine was raking in three and half million dollars a year in dividends alone.

Even by the inflated standards of her own time, that was more than enough motive for a murder in the minds of many people.

Now she was certain; greed not anger was behind Rafe Wilson's murder.

But even if Rafe had made such a valuable discovery, how would he go about obtaining the mineral rights?

First he'd have to make certain that his discovery was rich enough to make it worth his while. Wouldn't that necessitate a trip to the assayer's office?

Then, assuming the value of his find was confirmed, he'd need a financial backer. Someone who could afford to purchase the property. That must have meant some tricky negotiations on Rafe's part. If he divulged the location of the ore, why would his partner need him at all? And if he wouldn't disclose the location, how could his partner purchase the property?

Very tricky.

Still, it could be done if a person was wily enough. And from what Vera had heard about Verity's stepfather, he was cunning as well as mean. Such delicate negotiations wouldn't be beyond the realm of Rafe's abilities.

She slammed the journal closed and rose to her feet. Wiping her hands on her seat, she all but ran over to where Jericho was resting on the opposite side of the clearing. "We have to go back to Jerome," she announced.

His head jerked up. "Have you gone completely loco? Didn't we just get you out of town inches ahead of a lynch mob?"

"It can't be helped." She explained what she'd read in the journal and how she believed the assayer might have information that could help them uncover the business venture Rafe had been involved in.

Once they knew the location of his discovery, they could search the county records for the title holder of the property. Although Vera's plan offered scant hope for a solution, it was all they had.

"So you see," she finished, "we have to go back. The answers we need are in Jerome."

He jumped to his feet and pointed up the mountain. "Have you forgotten about that bushwhacker who's waiting for us with a loaded rifle?"

"No, but we'll have to go back by another path. It will never occur to him that we've doubled back on our trail. He'll be looking for us in Prescott. In the meantime we can take another route back up the mountain to Jerome."

Jericho stamped ineffectually at pitiful sagebrush clinging to life on the parched desert floor. "Woman, I have listened to your crazy stories. I've dressed you up and put you onstage. I've been in fistfights, been shot at and called a few choice names on your behalf. I haven't pressed you for the truth when I knew you were keeping secrets from me. I've bailed your sweet rear end out of more scrapes than could be expected of a man."

"But, Jericho, this is the last thing I'll ever ask of you. I promise."

"Hellfire, woman, I'm on the run for my life because of you! And you expect me to smile sweetly and haul us right back up the same mountainside we just spent two days coming down?"

"Please." It was all she could think of to say, but the weak plea seemed to have an effect on Jericho. The heated fire left his eyes and he drop-kicked a pebble that he apparently found offensive.

"I've got to be the biggest fool who ever pulled

on a pair of long pants,'' he muttered at last. ''I reckon we can take the old stage road back up. Save a few hours although that'll put us out in the open more.''

Vera raced for the jenny and mounted, for the first time not needing Jericho's laced fingers to boost herself up. ''Maybe we'll get enough head start while he looks for us in Prescott.''

Jericho paused, his hand on his pommel. ''Any reason we don't just wait for the back-shooter to come into town and nab him?''

''Because we don't know who we're looking for,'' she countered. ''And even if we recognized someone—like Jess Wiggins, for instance—we still won't have any proof that will hold up in court. We have to see the assayer and find out what Rafe and his partner were up to.''

Releasing a huge sigh of surrender, Jericho mounted. ''I'm really looking forward to another day or two in this saddle,'' he groused.

For her part, Vera was glad to have another day or two of freedom. Another few hours to bask in Jericho's company before she had to give him up for good.

STILL NOT QUITE believing he'd allowed Vera to talk him into riding back into the lions' den, Jericho clicked his tongue and led his horse up the dusty road.

He'd persuaded Vera to wait with his revolver outside town while he went into Prescott to trade the mules for a fresh horse for Vera. After he'd loaded up the supplies, he stopped for a short draft at the

Copper Queen Saloon and listened carefully to the gossip going around the bar.

No one mentioned the desperado, Verity McBride.

Nor was the late arrival of Deputy Hamblin a topic of conversation. The larger city was more concerned about the sudden drop in the price of copper ore and how it might affect their jobs.

Feeling momentarily relieved, Jericho drained his mug. Glancing around one last time to see if anyone familiar had followed him in, he nodded to the bartender and strolled outside into the sunlight.

Keeping a wary eye peeled to make sure no one trailed him out of town, Jericho moseyed slowly down the dusty street. He nodded and smiled to the passersby, hoping to foster the impression that he was just a normal traveler and didn't have a care in the world.

Vera was resting under the branches of a cottonwood, his Colt in her lap, when he rode up. Because the stage road was wider and far less torturous than the treacherous path they'd just taken, he knew they would make better time on the ascent by using horses. Pickings had been slim at the livery stable but he'd rustled up Boy-O, a decent-looking pinto gelding for Vera. Although tired from the ride down the mountain, Buckshot still looked better than any of the other nags the farrier had on hand.

As if glad to be on the move again, Vera was exceptionally agreeable as they started out. He chuckled to himself. No doubt she felt a tad guilty about manipulating him into going back to Jerome. Truth was, once he'd gotten over his initial shock at the suggestion, Jericho had his own reasons for wanting to return.

Henry Hamblin had been a good friend. Jericho didn't take his murder lightly. It galled him to think that a killer might go free. He'd been doing some thinking and it seemed to him that Jess Wiggins was the most likely villain. As soon as Jericho got Vera safely tucked away in his room again, he intended to track the big man down and demand his alibi for the times of the two killings.

At least it was a starting point.

Because they'd gotten such a late start, they only rode about two hours before Jericho pointed to a sheltered path off the main road. "There's an abandoned stage stop down there a piece. Good place as any to stay for the night. At least we'll be out of the weather."

When they drew up in front of the ramshackle structure, he was relieved to discover it was in better shape than he'd expected. Most of the windows were still intact, although they were so filthy he couldn't see through them.

Leaving Vera with the horses, he cautiously entered the cabin. He didn't want to stumble over a black bear waiting out the winter.

Other than the faint scurrying of a startled field mouse, the shack was deserted.

Not too bad, he thought as he uprighted a rickety wooden chair. The old bed frame was still in the corner although that mattress looked as if some furry creatures had been nesting in it. He lifted it off the bed, intending to take it outside for a good shaking.

He jumped back when a hissing sound caught his attention.

A hibernating rattler was expressing his anger at having his winter nap disturbed. Jericho inched away. He glanced around and found the remnants of an old broom resting against the fireplace.

Kicking the cabin door open with his foot, he yelled, "Take the horses and get back on the other side of the road."

"What's wrong?" Vera called back, her voice suddenly tense.

"You'll see. Just do it."

He didn't want to mention the rattler because she'd been acting so peculiar of late; he wouldn't be surprised if she screamed out loud like a city woman. When he heard the muffled shuffling of hooves crossing the road, he cautiously made his way back to the snake.

The rattling sound filled the cabin as the old fellow expressed his irritation. Jericho prodded him with the broomstick a couple times until the snake struck at it. In that split second when it came out of its coiled position. Jericho lunged forward, trapping the triangular head under the scratchy broom straws.

Writhing and twisting like a mad thing, the rattler struggled but the broom held it firmly in place. Stepping carefully around the edge of the bedstead, Jericho reached down and grasped the creature firmly behind its head.

Using both hands he gingerly held it at arm's length as he slowly crossed the cabin floor and stepped into the fading daylight. He heard Vera's sharp intake of breath but to her credit, she didn't scream. He carried the yard-long diamondback a good half mile from the cabin and hefted it over a waist-high boulder.

It hit the ground, hissed at the rock and slithered away in the opposite direction.

Only then did Jericho let out a relieved breath. Good thing he'd decided to air out that old mattress or they might have had a more uncomfortable night than he'd counted on.

By the time he returned to the cabin, Vera had led the horses over to the small corral and was in the process of uncinching Boy-O's saddle. He helped her with the heavy task and then went around the corral checking the pickets and hammering a few more firmly into the ground.

Finally, their outdoor chores done, they carried the saddlebags back into the shack. While Vera swept mouse droppings off the dirt floor and generally tidied up, Jericho hauled in firewood and soon had a blaze flaring in the huge fireplace. Maybe too big a blaze, he thought, loosening the first button on his shirt.

He fixed them a simple meal of smoked ham and eggs, and broke open a crusty loaf of homemade bread he'd bartered for at a café in Prescott. When they'd eaten their fill and scrubbed off their tin plates, he settled back on the single chair while Vera huddled on the bed, wrapping her arms around her knees.

Now that they had no busywork to occupy their attention, the silence between them was deafening.

Jericho sipped his coffee. "You ever going to tell me what's got your drawers in such a knot?"

Her head jerked up. "I'm not upset, if that's what you're implying."

"What I'm implying is that I don't understand the hot-cold treatment you're giving me. I mean, you sure as hell weren't pushing me out of your bedroll last night but today you act like I've got leprosy or something. I think I deserve an explanation."

"I, uh, just…it's so complicated. I'm not sure how to make you understand."

He slammed the chair onto all four legs with a furious bang. "Try speaking English! Hell, I'm not as all-fired stupid as you seem to think I am. Give me your complicated explanation in simple sentences. I'll study on it and try my best, ma'am, to understand," he finished with a sarcastic flourish.

Vera picked at the holey saddle blanket covering the filthy mattress.

"You owe me the truth, at least," he said quietly.

She owed him her life several times over, she ruefully acknowledged. And he deserved better than she'd given him. He thought she was mocking his intelligence, but in truth, her own intellect was strained trying to comprehend the metaphysical events that had transpired over the last few days.

"You're not going to believe me," she said at last.

"Maybe not, but give it a shot."

Closing her eyes, Vera leaned against the wall, barely feeling the cold air that seeped between the cracked chinking. Where should she start? At the beginning, she thought. Wasn't that what they always told their suspects during questioning? Just keep it simple and start at the beginning.

"Remember I told you that I was a highway patrol officer in California?"

"Yeah, I recall you saying something like that. Never knew what you meant by it, though."

"I mean I'm like a police officer except I mostly ride around in a squad car and stop people for speeding, drunk driving and expired license plates."

He slowly shook his head. "I don't have any idea what you're talking about."

Her voice raised in exasperation. "That's what I meant about not being able to explain. Okay, listen, try to keep an open mind and don't interrupt until I finish. Okay?"

He nodded. "Go on."

Taking a deep breath, she plunged into the incredible story. "My name is Vera McBride—not Verity, and I was born in 1969. I'm almost thirty years old. I was here on vacation, I wanted to find out something about one of my ancestors, Verity McBride. Believe it or not, Jerome is a popular tourist destination in my time. All those buildings are now gift shops and museums. Of course, they're not the same buildings because Jerome is going to burn almost to the ground twice in the next few years and—"

She broke off at the bewildered look on his face. She was going too fast and giving him too much unbelievable detail.

Deliberately slowing the pace of her narrative, she continued. "Anyway, I was touring the old Balbriggan Mine when a rotted timber gave way and I fell into an old shaft."

"Which is where I found you," he blurted, as if

relieved that she'd finally said something he could relate to.

"That's right. But somehow during that fall, I'd...I'd traveled through time. And don't tell me that's impossible," she warned when he started to shake his head. "I'm the living proof that it is!"

"If you say so."

Vera knew she wasn't getting through to him but she plunged on anyway. He'd insisted upon the truth, and now he could just sit there and hear it.

"All my life I've been told that I bear an uncanny resemblance to Verity. I was even named after her. So when I came to in Verity's world, you mistook me for her."

"You *are* Verity," he stated bluntly.

"No, I'm not!" Vera rose from the bed and crossed the room to kneel in front of him on the dirt floor. "Look at me, Jericho, truly look. I don't have as much Indian blood in my veins as Verity, don't you see it? My eyes are lighter, my hair has a bit more curl. My cheekbones aren't as great as hers. I'm almost ten years older than the woman you know. Don't you see the differences?"

He stared intently into her face, taking her chin in his hands, turning her head one way and then another. "I'm trying to make sense out of what you're telling me. And, truth is, you *do* look different than when I was talking to you in the kitchen the other night. But, Vera, traveling through time? Do you honestly expect me to believe that? You're tired and weary from worrying about the outcome of your trial, that's why you look a bit older."

And why you're so confused, lay unspoken in the air between them.

Tossing her head in frustration, she stalked to the bed and opened her backpack. She pulled her driver's license and credit cards out of her wallet and carried them back to Jericho. "Look. Read this. It says right here that my name is Vera Elaine McBride. It gives my date of birth and my address. Read it!"

Jericho took the plasticized cards from her and flicked them with his fingernail. "What're these things made of?"

"Plastic. It hasn't been invented yet in your time."

"Uh-huh." He scanned the writing on her license and squinted closely at the photograph. Holding it before the flickering firelight, he moved the card back and forth. Vera realized he'd just noticed the holographic image that prevented the license from being altered.

"Where'd you get this?" he asked at last. "And what're these other things?"

"Credit cards. Mostly maxed out."

He shrugged. "You're talking Latin again."

Perching on the edge of the wobbly table, she squarely faced him. "In my time people don't use cash much for major purchases. Or even small ones. The store or bank issues you one of these cards so you can buy merchandise and pay for it later. A little at a time if you like."

His eyes lit up in comprehension. "Like running a tab at the bar or the general store."

"That's exactly right! Except this is all done by computer and—"

"What's a computer?"

"It's a machine that holds as much information as an entire library."

"Hmmmph. That's something. What are some other things in your...your place you live."

Excited now that he finally seemed to be listening, and maybe even believing, Vera launched into a dramatic telling of life in San Francisco. She talked about the cable cars, about the hilly streets, the tourists, BART, the culturally diverse population, about the crowded airport and rush hour traffic on the Golden Gate Bridge.

Jericho shook his head. "I heard where Henry Ford invented one of those motor cars you're talking about, but I'm not quite sure I understand how those big machines full of people get off the ground to fly through the air."

Vera realized she'd once more gone too deeply into her explanation. "Let me show you something else."

She ran across the cabin and retrieved her canister of pepper spray. "Women and police officers carry this stuff. I can't show you what it does, but if I pressed this nozzle, it would spray you with a blinding mixture of chemicals and hot pepper juice."

Jericho jumped to his feet and threw the cards onto the table beside her. "What kind of weak-minded fool do you take me for? Did you think I've never been out of this town in my life? Never seen a perfume atomizer? I don't know where you got all this stuff, but I've seen magic shows and tricksters hawking their wares before."

"No! It's no trick, Jericho. Please, you have to believe me."

"All I believe is that I was wrong about you all along. I don't know what kind of swindle you're trying to put over on me, but it isn't going to work."

He grabbed his hat and stalked outside into the cold winter night.

Chapter Fourteen

Jericho stomped the ground, wrapping his arms across his chest to ward off the evil cold. He wished he'd had the good sense to grab his coat when he'd stormed out of the cabin or the good sense to buy a pint of whiskey in Prescott.

But, most of all, he wished he'd had the good sense not to get involved with that devilish woman in the first place.

He'd known her for a long time and he'd never taken her for a liar or a cheat, but what else explained those phony, ridiculous credentials she was carrying?

No more stops, he decided. They'd ride all night if they had to, but the sooner he got her back to Jerome and they cleared up this mess—even if it turned out she was guilty of Rafe's murder—the sooner he could get her back to the Apaches. His debt to Min-e-wah would be repaid in full and he'd finally be shed of Verity and her craziness.

And good riddance.

He was damned lucky he'd discovered her lunacy and her duplicity before it was too late.

But something growled deep inside that it was already too late. He'd already crossed some invisible line that made him susceptible to Vera despite her obvious chicanery.

For the life of him, though, Jericho couldn't figure out what she hoped to gain by her preposterous tale.

Unless...unless it was true.

Could she really have made up all those incredible tales? Vessels that carried hundreds of people flying through the air faster than the swiftest eagle. Cities where people lived in huge buildings holding thousands of residents who made their way through these cities by underground trains. Incredible. Unbelievable.

Still...

An icy wind swept through the clearing, cutting through his thin shirt and chilling him to the bone and slapping him back to reality. What had he been thinking? Of course she'd made up those preposterous tales.

Gritting his teeth, Jericho set his jaw and stalked back into the cabin.

THE RIDE BACK TO JEROME was tense but uneventful. Except for basic necessities, they didn't exchange a word. Even those essential utterances were cold and barely civil.

It was after dark by the time they reached the outskirts of town. Once again, Jericho led them down the narrow alley that ran behind the Copper Penny. Feeling like a hapless catfish being reeled in to its sad fate, Vera once more followed him up the back stairs of the building to his rooms.

He'd stubbornly refused to take half of the narrow bed the previous evening, choosing instead to sleep on the floor in front of the fire. Vera knew he must be exhausted. He was still angry at what he perceived to be her fraudulent story; his teeth were clenched so tightly his jaws must be sore. The tension radiating from his stiff shoulders was almost palpable.

In an attempt to soothe the charged atmosphere, she said quietly, "I think you should take the bedroom tonight. I'll sleep out here."

"No. I've got to go downstairs. I still have a business to run and I have some errands to attend to first thing in the morning. You take the bedroom so I won't have to be concerned about disturbing you."

What disturbed her was the coldly formal tone he now took whenever he was forced to address her directly. Even though she intellectually understood his reasons for withdrawing, she felt as if a vital life-sustaining force had been taken from her. She wanted the old good-natured Jericho back.

"All right," she answered at length, not wanting to provoke another argument.

"What would you like me to bring up for dinner?" he asked.

He might hate her guts but his genteel manner demanded he not abandon his duties as her host. That icy ability to withdraw so completely, while still treating her with great courtesy, hurt worse than if he'd stomped his feet and shouted. At least she could have shouted back. There was no way to combat indifference.

"Nothing. I'm not hungry." The churning in her

stomach wouldn't allow for food. All she wanted was a good night's sleep so she could tackle the assayer in the morning. Once the truth of Rafe's death was disclosed, she was going to pour her energies into finding her way back to the future.

"As you wish." Jericho inclined his head slightly. "I'll see you in the morning, then."

He closed the door softly behind him.

She resisted a sudden urge to plant her foot on his backside and help him down the hallway.

Feeling hurt and disgruntled by his unfair refusal to even consider the possibility that she might be telling the truth, Vera stalked into the bedroom, shedding her dirty clothing as she walked. Jericho's frosty emotional distance was harder to endure than his occasional displays of temper.

She understood his bewilderment and sense of betrayal but there was nothing she could say or do to alleviate his distrust and disbelief.

Nor could she alleviate the wrenching sense of loss she felt since he'd turned away from her.

If he'd truly cared about her, he would trust her. Believe her. No matter how preposterous her story might sound at first.

Not bothering to find a clean nightshirt, Vera flopped naked onto the bed and pulled the comforter up under her chin. In seconds she fell into a deep sleep, and dreamed of her cat Squiggles, who was chasing a snake down a mine shaft.

In her dream, Squiggles morphed into Jericho who grinned at her like the Cheshire cat from Alice's

Wonderland. "Liar, liar," he hissed at her before darting off down the rabbit hole.

SUNLIGHT WAS STREAMING through the filmy curtains when Vera was awakened by pounding on the bedroom door.

She struggled to sit up and realized with a start that she was nude. She yanked the linen sheet over her bosom just as the bedroom door opened wide.

"Yoo-hoo! Miz LaFleur, you awake in here?" Susannah Sweet's bright red head peeked around the door. "Oh, good, you're up. Mr. Jackson sent me up with a breakfast tray for you. You need to eat up 'cause ole Gus is going to be filling the tub so's you can have a bath. Mr. Jackson says you need one."

Fine, Vera grumped to herself. Now he was hinting that she smelled. Actually, she thought as she adjusted the covers, a faint twang of horsy aroma *was* clinging to her skin. She refused to entertain the notion that Jericho was just being thoughtful, though.

Susannah set the heavily loaded breakfast tray on the bedside table. Chattering incessantly, she revealed how Mr. Jackson was in some kind of mood this morning. "I'm telling you, he near about bit the heads off half the people he talked to this morning. Actin' meaner 'n a snake, he is."

Susannah paused and gave Vera a frankly assessing gaze. "Acts like a man in love iffen you ask me."

Vera laughed out loud. "If you're referring to me, you couldn't be further from the truth. The only thing Jericho would love about me is to see me gone."

"Maybe so. But even as riled as he is, he made

sure that you were tended to. Breakfast, bath water, even sent Sally over to the mercantile to fetch you some clean street clothes. She should be back any time.''

Vera was surprised he'd revealed her presence to any of his employees. As if reading her mind, Susannah quickly reassured her. ''He told us he'd see us in hell iffen either of us let slip that you was here.''

Uncovering the bountiful breakfast tray, the redhead set it on the bed beside Vera and sashayed back to the door. ''You kin think what you want, Miz LaFleur, but Mr. Jackson sets great store by you. Most of us wouldn't take it kindly iffen you was to betray his esteem.''

With that, the saloon waitress disappeared out the door.

An hour later, feeling greatly replenished by the food, hot bath and fresh clothing, Vera pulled the hood of her new brown velvet bonnet over her face. She stood in front of the mirror and straightened the lilac-sprigged muslin dress. Satisfied that the bonnet successfully shaded her features from casual view, she slipped out Jericho's door and down the back staircase.

A few moments later, she stood in front of the office of J. P. Gilmore, Assayer. According to the gold-leafed sign painted on the frosted window, he would open his doors for business at eleven o'clock.

She didn't wait long before a dapper man in a gray-striped business suit and bowler hat clattered down the wooden sidewalk in her direction. When he drew abreast of her, he tipped his hat. "Madam, are you waiting for me? My apologies."

Clearly unaccustomed to dealing with women in his trade, J. P. Gilmore kept giving her curious glances as he ushered her into the dim interior.

"Please, madam, have a seat while I draw the shades."

Vera settled into a wooden armchair and watched the slightly built man flutter around the small space. He yanked open the shades on both windows, feather dusted the ledge in front of his cubicle and finally, took off his jacket and hung it on the coat rack by the door. Turning to face her, he smiled brightly.

"Now, my good woman, how can I be of assistance?"

Clearly, J. P. Gilmore was open for business.

While she'd been soaking in the tin bathtub, Vera had concocted a cover story of sorts. Smiling effusively at the rattled man, she dabbed her cheek with a lacy hanky she'd found in Jericho's bureau.

"Mr. Gilmore, is it?"

"Yes, madam, and you are…?"

"Oh! I'm sorry. Silly me, I plumb forgot myself." Falling into her chosen role, Vera had to suppress a smile at the honey-dripping Southern accent that flowed easily from her lips. She raised a gloved hand and allowed the assayer to touch it before pulling it demurely back to her lap. "My name is…Ethel. Ethel Wilson. Perhaps you knew my dear departed brother, Rafe?"

"Oh my," J. P. Gilmore blanched. "My dear lady, I am so sorry at your loss. Why I had no idea Mr.

Wilson had family outside Jerome, much less a sister of such obvious fine breeding. May I welcome you to our town and offer *any* assistance you might require?"

"Surely," she murmured. What she was going to need was a barf bag if he didn't lighten up on the genteel charm.

"Mr. Gilmore—"

"Please, call me J.P. We're very informal out here in the Wild West." He scurried behind his desk and dragged his chair across the room, placing it directly in front of her so their knees were almost touching.

"All right, J.P. Anyway, I understand that my brother was involved in a...business venture that you might have some information about."

"Oh, me. I don't believe I can...you see, I guarantee my customers complete confidence. If I were to...reveal details about their discoveries, claim jumping and all manner of violence might commence. A man in my position has to be very circumspect."

Dabbing her eyes with the hanky one more time for good measure, she reached across the short distance and patted his knee. The small man shivered visibly and coughed as a bright pink tinge lit his pale cheeks.

"Mr. Gilmore, J.P. I certainly appreciate your reticence to betray a confidence. Indeed I applaud your circumcision—er, circumspection. But, you see, my dear brother borrowed a sum of money from me to fund his enterprise. And he promised me that my investment would be completely protected. Unfortunately, he died before he could complete the necessary paperwork.''

"Oh, my dear, Miss— Is it Miss, by the way?"

"Missus." Seeing the crestfallen look on his face, she quickly added, "I'm a widow, you see. That's why it was necessary for me to ascertain that this investment was sound." Vera sniffled loudly. "I loaned my brother almost every penny my sainted husband left to me."

J.P. leaned forward and tentatively patted her arm. "Oh, you poor lady. To lose your husband and your brother at such a young age. How distressful. And, of course, I completely understand your need to, er, untangle your brother's business affairs. Now, how can I help you?"

"Rafe didn't want to…clutter my head with details, you understand, but I understand his business venture involved some sort of mining? Copper, perhaps."

Gilmore shook his head, his thin hair flapping with the motion. "No, not copper. Mr. Wilson did come in with an ore sample some months ago—a very nice chunk of ore with a vein of nearly pure silver. Quite a find."

Silver! Verity's journal had mentioned silver.

Certain that she was on the right trail at last, Vera played out her hand. Clutching the hanky to her bosom, she exhaled, watching J. P. Gilmore's eyes widen at the spectacle. "My gracious, silver, you say. Did my brother happen to mention where this vein of silver might be located?"

"What?" Gilmore reluctantly lifted his gaze from

her chest. "No. No, he didn't. In fact, it would have been quite foolish of him to divulge that kind of information until he'd completed all the formalities of acquisition. And, of course, he didn't do that before his death or you would have been informed. As principle investor."

Smiling widely to cover her disappointment, she fingered her hanky. "I see. Well you've been most helpful, J.P."

She stood up and fluffed her skirts, trying to think of any more information she might be able to elicit from the randy assayer.

"Will you be staying long in our fair city?" he asked as he accompanied her to the door.

She waved her hanky. "I just couldn't say. So much depends on how long it takes me to unravel my dear brother's estate. My funds are quite limited now, you understand."

Taking severe liberties, he patted her shoulder and yanked his hand away as if he'd been slapped. "I certainly do understand. Perhaps you'll allow me to escort you to dinner at the Gilbert Hotel one evening during your stay? They serve an excellent Delmonico steak on Friday nights."

"That would be just lovely, Mr. Gil—er, J.P."

Beaming with pleasure, he opened the door. "I look forward to meeting with you again, then, Mrs. Wilson."

"Please, call me Edith."

He drew back. "I thought you said Ethel?"

Busted. To cover her gaffe, she effected a nervous titter. "My mother named me after a pair of great aunts, Ethel and Edith. I answer to either one. Or both.''

''Well that's very…unusual. Ethel-Edith.''

Smiling broadly, she stepped down the wooden sidewalk a few paces. ''My family *is* quite unusual. Until Friday, J.P.''

''Until Friday.''

He closed the door behind him only to open it a moment later. ''Oh! Ethel-Edith! Just a moment.''

She paused while he trotted down the sidewalk.

''I thought of something that might help you,'' he panted as he came abreast of her.

''Oh, and what might that be?'' she simpered in her broadest Southern patois.

''Rafe Wilson would have had to file a claim if he'd discovered a silver deposit. They'll have records at the county court.''

Vera's heart sank. Of course. The county court in Prescott. Nearly a two-day ride away. The place she'd just left.

She'd hit another stone wall.

After once more offering J. P. Gilmore her profuse thanks, she made her escape and started back to the Copper Penny.

There had to be some way to discover who'd actually filed the claim on Rafe's silver stake without riding all the way to Prescott. But how?

At that moment, she spotted Jess Wiggins sitting on a bench outside the mercantile. He was whittling on a piece of wood, idly watching the passersby. Vera ducked her head and paused to admire a bolt of fabric in the window. If Jess Wiggins caught even a glimpse of her face he was bound to recognize her. She couldn't take the chance.

Keeping her back to him, she sidestepped a pile of horse apples and hurried across the main street. Stepping back onto the wooden sidewalk, she found herself directly in front of the telegraph office.

Of course!

Peering in the dust-streaked window, she saw the telegraph agent standing at a counter, skimming a newspaper. Casting a leery glance at Jess Wiggins who appeared to be taking no notice of her actions, she stepped inside.

"Good morning." The telegrapher looked up and folded his newspaper. An engraved metal plate on the counter identified him as Marvin Shott.

"Good morning, sir." Not in the mood for another flirtation, she kept her tone crisp and businesslike.

"Did you want to send a wire, ma'am?"

"No, not exactly." She slowly approached the counter, deciding what tact to take. The widowed sister had worked so well with the assayer, she decided to stick with it.

Launching into her story of being Rafe Wilson's impoverished sister, she concluded, "So you see, I'm trying to gather any information I can on my brother's holdings to assist our attorneys in straightening out this dreadful mess."

Marvin Shott smiled affably. "I'm sorry to say that I have utter sympathy for your position. Rafe Wilson wasn't a...shall we say...a highly organized man."

"Oh, you *do* understand. Is there any way you can help me?"

"Me? What on earth could I know of Rafe Wilson's business affairs?"

She sighed in frustration. She'd been clutching at straws; of course this man wouldn't know anything about Rafe's silver mine. "Since all the records are in Prescott, I thought perhaps he might have sent a telegram or somehow filed his claim by wire but I guess..."

Shott bit his lip and shook his head sorrowfully. "No, I'm afraid that would have to be done in person. But Rafe *did* send a telegram once. I remember it quite clearly."

"Is that so?" She leaned on the counter, willing him to reveal more.

"Let's see now." He reached for a wooden box under the counter and riffled through a stack of papers. "That would have been late July, early August. I remember it being not too much after our Independence Day celebration. Let me see... Ah! Here it is. Yes."

He shoved the paper across the counter.

Trying to still the excited trembling in her fingers, Vera picked up the pale yellow pages.

To: Yavapai County Records Clerk
County Courthouse
Prescott, Arizona
Need to discover ownership status of abandoned mind. Stop. Can this be researched by wire? Stop. Please reply soon. Stop. Very important. Stop.
Wilson, Jerome, Arizona.

The responding reply was clipped to the yellow paper. The Yavapai County Records Clerk had said simply, "No. Stop. Must be done at Prescott Courthouse. Stop."

So that was that.

She handed the papers back to the telegrapher. "Thanks so much for your help. I guess I'll have to head back to Prescott. It's just such a long trip in this weather."

He nodded. "I heard this morning that some state dignitary is coming up from the valley tomorrow, so they'll be opening the railroad for him since there isn't any snow on the tracks. You can probably ride back down and save yourself a full day or better."

Grateful for that good news at least, Vera bade him good day.

As she slowly walked down the sidewalk, she glanced across the street. Jess Wiggins was gone. Glancing around fearfully, she hurried her steps until she reached the Copper Penny. Drawing a relieved breath, she rushed around back and raced up the stairs to the safety of Jericho's apartment.

She called out, but Jericho apparently hadn't returned yet. Although it hurt her to be in the same room with him, knowing all the while that their time together was so very limited, she wished with all her heart that he was here now. Besides cheering her with his gentle smile and easygoing manner, she would have liked to bounce her thoughts off him. He knew the way things were done in these parts and his insight would prove invaluable.

But she had no idea when he'd return and she had

an instinctive awareness that time was rapidly running out. She'd have to continue sorting this out on her own. Dropping her bonnet on the settee, she sank into one of the stiff-backed armchairs and thought over the information she'd gleaned.

Rafe Wilson had discovered a deposit of nearly pure silver.

Silver was mentioned more than once in Verity's journal.

Vera ran into the bedroom, grabbed the journal from the nightstand drawer and flopped on the bed. Flipping the dog-eared pages, she ran her finger down the unlined pages with their lopsided, uneven cursive until she found the reference she was looking for. The night her baby brother was born, Verity went looking for Rafe at the Balbriggan Mine. That's where she first said something about silver shoes hanging on a post.

Turning the pages, Vera found a second mention of silver. Again, referenced in the same passage as the Balbriggan. Furthermore, Verity's journal had been found in a pit at the bottom of that same abandoned mine.

Rafe had asked the Yavapai Records Clerk about a title search for an old mine. That mine, she was dead certain, was the Balbriggan.

That's where the answers waited.

And that's where she had to go.

But not dressed like a calico princess.

Vera looked around for her soiled jeans and was pleasantly surprised to see her clothing, freshly washed and folded neatly on the side chair.

She changed quickly and laced up her Nikes. Grabbing the hairbrush from the dressing stand, she took a few quick swipes and tied her hair in a ponytail with the bright red bandanna. Hopefully she wouldn't run into anyone who might look askance at her attire. Taking only enough time to scribble a note for Jericho, she picked up her backpack and hurried across the room, wondering if there was anything she'd forgotten.

She pulled open the heavy door and gasped. "Oh!"

Dr. Greavy stood on the threshold, his hand poised in midair.

"You startled me," she said.

"Sorry." Doc Greavy chuckled. "I didn't have time to knock when you yanked open the door. You look like you're going someplace in an all-fired hurry." He sent her clothes a curious glance. "Quite frankly, I'm surprised to find you here. I thought you'd accompanied Deputy Hamblin to Prescott."

Vera forced herself to slow down, to take the time to respond in a courteous manner. He already knew her "real" identity; there was no sense arousing his further suspicions.

"I was just going out for some fresh air."

"So, things were cleared up in Prescott? They released you?"

"Temporarily," she prevaricated. "I have to go back for the trial."

"I see. Is Jericho available?"

She tossed her head, wishing the doctor would go away so she could start the long ride to the Balbriggan. She didn't want to be in that eerie old mine after dark. "He's not here. You could ask downstairs. They might have a better idea when to expect him."

"I'll do that." The physician nodded and started for the staircase but paused at the railing. "I was so startled to see you that I almost forgot to ask. How are you feeling these days? Did that sleeping potion help any?"

She'd almost forgotten the sleeping draft he'd prescribed since she'd only taken it one night. But she didn't want to take the time for a long-winded explanation so she merely nodded. "Helps a lot, Doctor. I certainly appreciate everything you've done."

"No problem, young lady. I hope everything turns out well for you."

"Thank you."

He nodded again and slowly descended the staircase.

Vera waited until he was out of sight before she darted for the back stairs. When she emerged in the alley, she glanced around and made her way to the main street and headed for the livery stable.

Just as she reached the large brick-red structure, one of the few painted buildings in Jerome, she thought she saw Jess Wiggins slip into a doorway across the street.

Praying he hadn't noticed her, she stepped inside the stable and inhaled the clean scent of fresh hay. While she looked around for the blacksmith, she suddenly realized she had no idea how to go about renting a horse. Were they let by the day or by the hour? And how much should she expect to pay?

Not that it mattered. She didn't have any money that wouldn't look counterfeit to the blacksmith.

Vera glanced down the length of the dim stable. A young man was currying Boy-O, the pinto she'd ridden from Prescott. Buckshot, however, was in the first stall by the door.

That's when she decided her only recourse was to steal Jericho's horse.

Chapter Fifteen

Why wouldn't she listen to him? Why did he have to fall for the most pigheaded, iron-willed, and cantankerous woman inflicted upon mankind since Eve fled the Garden? If Jericho had the sense God gave this miserable mule, he'd turn around and head back to Jerome.

Although he'd now come to accept the incredible fact that Vera wasn't Verity, and that she came from a more sophisticated place in the distant future and had superior knowledge of almost everything, he knew she was no match for the cold-blooded killer who was out to destroy her. Jericho might not know about the wonders of Vera's world, but he knew about men. And this one had to be stopped.

When he'd gone to the livery stable, he was stunned to discover that Boy-O had been rented and some horse thief had apparently "borrowed" Buckshot. That horse thief, he was certain, had a long black ponytail and the sweetest lips he'd ever tasted.

He couldn't wait to get his hands on her. Sweat popped on his forehead at the memory of the last time his hands had roamed her luscious body. Jericho slapped the leather reins across his own thigh in a failed effort to banish the sensual reminder.

Minnie, the smithy's own mule, rounded a narrow corner and stopped abruptly. They were at the clearing beside the Balbriggan line shack. The deserted shanty stood dark, deserted. Jericho's eyes carefully surveyed the perimeter of the clearing. No sign of Vera. No sign of any life. It sickened him to think what that might mean.

Had the killer already found her on the trail? Jericho had no illusions that if she was captured, her pursuer meant to silence her. Permanently.

Giving Minnie a nudge with his toe, he kept his eyes peeled as he negotiated the exposed clearing. Stopping in front of the shack, he had one leg on the ground when he heard a muffled sound behind him. He jerked around in time to catch a glimpse of a rifle butt whishing through the air toward his head.

A second later a slashing pain lanced his temple and the world went black.

THROUGH A PAIN-FILLED haze, Jericho had a sense of being dragged across the dirt clearing. He grunted once as a rock embedded in the packed soil struck his cheekbone. Blessed darkness enveloped him again.

Minutes or hours later he groggily emerged from the shrouded gray world that had been his merciful guardian. Burning pain wracked his shoulders and wrists, while a dull ache along his cheekbone greeted his awakening.

He tried to sit up and discovered the worst agony had been saved for last. His head felt as if a dozen miners, iron pick axes in hand, were digging for precious minerals inside his skull. White-hot and sharp, the pain stabbed him again and again.

After a few moments he found he could open his eyes if he didn't move his head. Like a morning-after drunk, Jericho kept his head perfectly still while he surveyed his surroundings.

The flickering light of an oil lantern hanging on a piling offered a dim image of his prison. He was tethered to a thick post like a lamb set out as bait for a pack of marauding wolves. As his eyes adjusted to the frail light, Jericho saw that he was in the abandoned mine. Very near the dangerous shaft from which he'd first hauled Vera to safety.

But Jericho wasn't alone.

His jailer's shadow danced in the lamplight as he cheerily went about his business. "So, you're awake? Too bad. Would've been better if you'd slept right through to eternity."

He moved slightly and Jericho saw the huge bundle of dynamite sticks his captor had lashed to an overhead beam. He'd used enough explosive to blow up half of the mountainside.

Catching Jericho's wide-eyed stare, he laughed, a phlegmy chortle that made Jericho's blood run cold.

"Just a little surprise for your lady friend. Maybe we should have a ceremony; let you lovebirds stay together until death do you part. Which is going to be real soon, old friend."

Jericho spat at the man's feet. "You're no friend of mine, you slimy bastard. You won't get away with this."

"Right. I'm quivering with fear."

Jericho squirmed against the ropes that were eating into his wrists but knew the struggle was futile. When Vera arrived, they were both doomed.

VERA WIPED A BEAD of sweat from her forehead and sighed with relief as Buckshot trotted into the clearing in front of the mine. Accustomed to real estate dissected by marked roads, streets and freeways, she'd gotten lost at least three times during her meandering journey along the unmarked mountain trails. But she finally made it.

She still didn't understand how this time travel stuff worked, but the answer, along with the vein of silver Rafe discovered, was in the Balbriggan mine. Of that, Vera was certain.

Dismounting, she tied Jericho's horse to a mesquite shrub and started toward the mine entrance. She stopped short. On the edge of the clearing, almost hidden by a huge scrub oak, Boy-O, the pinto gelding, was tethered beside a large gray mule.

Reaching into her backpack, Vera pulled out the canister of pepper spray and gingerly walked toward the timber-framed opening. Suppressing a shudder as she recalled the last time she'd entered this mine, she drew in a deep breath and stepped forward, leaving the sunlight behind.

She paused inside, allowing time for her vision to adjust to the dark and musty cavern. In the distance she heard the murmur of masculine voices. Who, she wondered, was in here with Jericho? And why?

Instinctively, she knew the answer didn't bode well.

Inching down the dirt-floored corridor, she followed the sound of their voices, praying she wouldn't get lost or, God forbid, fall through another rotted timber. The intermittent voices grew louder until she could actually pick up a word here and there.

Vera slowed her pace knowing she was closing in on the other occupants.

When she came to a fork in the mazelike interior, she took a few tentative steps down the right passageway and was rewarded by the flickering glow cast by a lantern just around the next bend. Easing forward, step by cautious step, she paused and leaned against the rammed-earth wall, hoping the dreadful pounding of her heart wasn't audible to the men only a few feet away.

Keeping her finger on the pepper spray nozzle, she poked her head around the corner. Jericho was bound to a beam a few feet from where the lantern's beam glimmered on a bright silver horseshoe.

The meaning behind the reference in Verity's journal to the "silver shoe" was suddenly as clear as the fear pounding through her breast. That silver horse shoe must be the conduit for passage through time.

Vera had a sudden distinct memory of clutching something metallic just before she fell through the rotted floor and hurtled through time.

Had Verity somehow discovered the special horse shoe and visited the future?

Vera smiled, feeling a surge of kinship with the ancestor she'd never met. Maybe Verity *had* been watching out for her namesake all these years after all.

Right now, though, Vera's ancestral guardian wasn't in sight and Jericho was in trouble. A shadow moved and she jerked back around the corner. Someone was with him, she'd already known that, but who?

The who, she realized, didn't really matter. Someone, probably the same man who'd killed Rafe Wilson and the deputy, had taken Jericho by surprise. Vera had no illusions that the unseen murderer wanted her—the woman he believed to be Verity—dead. He was waiting for her arrival.

Gripping the pepper spray, Vera drew in a deep breath. No sense keeping him waiting any longer.

She stepped around the corner.

Rafe Wilson's killer had his back to her. He was bent over fiddling with something out of her line of vision. Holding the cylinder at arm's length, Vera decided her best chance to take him by surprise was to wait quietly until he turned around. Before he could recover from seeing her, she'd squirt him in the face with the chemical spray.

As if sensing her thoughts, the man straightened slowly then turned around and squarely faced her.

In her shock, Vera almost dropped the spray.

Doc Greavy!

A wide, evil grin split the man's moon-shaped face. "Why, Miz McBride, you act surprised. You were expecting President Cleveland, perhaps?"

Yet after the initial shock, his identity made perfect sense. Rafe Wilson had no money; his partner would have had to supply the financial backing. His partner would have moved in more sophisticated social circles where he could enlist the supporters their enterprise would require.

Why hadn't she seen all this before? Some detective she made, wasting so much time concentrating on Jess Wiggins.

It wasn't too late. She hoped.

Vera raised the spray container. "Cut him loose. Now."

Greavy laughed. "Or you'll what, young lady?"

She shook the canister. "This contains a mixture of chemicals and fiery red peppers. If I spray it into your eyes, you'll think they're on fire."

"Oh, my. Are you a devotee of that new author, Jules Verne?" He chuckled.

Before she could respond, he flicked a wooden match and whirled around.

A tiny hissing sound sizzled through the air. At first Vera thought they'd disturbed a rattlesnake, but then the doctor moved aside and she saw what he'd done.

He'd ignited a long section of fusing. Its white glow burned steadily toward a bundle of dynamite nestled in the rafter above Jericho's head.

At that moment, Greavy charged her. Vera reacted instinctively, pressing the nozzle of the pepper spray. She watched in horror as the jet of burning liquid shot across the short distance—straight into Greavy's eyes.

The large man screamed, a bleating sound like a gargantuan pig being butchered. Hands covering his face, he knocked her to the ground in his mad rush for the cave entrance.

She hit her head with a solid thunk on the packed dirt floor but she held on to consciousness, knowing if she let go she and Jericho would surely die.

Vera felt woozy as she rolled over and stared, unseeing, at Jericho. Only his calm voice filtered through her groggy mind. "Vera, honey, you have to get out of here. Come on, get up. You have to get to safety."

Suddenly comprehending, she willed her eyes to focus and stared at the burning fuse. The long skinny wick sparked brightly in the faint light.

How much time did they have? How long would it take that fuse to burn down? A minute—two? Did she have enough time to free Jericho and still get to that silver horse shoe?

"Get out of here!" Jericho's voice had lost its quiet patience.

"I can't leave you." She stared at his beloved face, a stream of blood flowing down his cheek. It was true, she realized with a sinking heart. She couldn't abandon this man who'd taught her what life was truly about.

"Save yourself!"

Time seemed suspended as Vera absorbed his unselfish words. Yes, she could very likely make her own escape from the mine before the explosion. Perhaps even free Jericho as well. Maybe. But if the mine blew up Vera knew she'd never be able to yank on that silver horse shoe. Never find her way back to her own time.

The choice was simple and devastating.

Jericho or her own future.

The hissing wick spat, taunting her with its steady progress toward the dynamite.

Suddenly, Vera understood the strange longings that had twisted her apart these past few days. She'd fallen in love with Jericho Jackson. To trade his life for hers was unthinkable. There was no future without him. In any century.

Startled into action, she dashed forward, fumbling with the tight knots that bound him to the beam. Somehow she managed to free him. But when he tried to stand, his knees wobbled beneath him.

She glanced at the wick. More than half the original length was gone. Hurry, they had to hurry.

Wordlessly, she slipped an arm around his waist. With his forearm draped around her shoulder they started a slow, halting progress toward the mine entrance.

Finally, Vera spotted daylight at the end of the long corridor and knew they'd almost made it. Safety lay fifty feet ahead.

Then she tripped on a large, inert bundle blocking their path. Glancing down she saw Doc Greavy lying unconscious on the dirt floor. In his temporary blindness, he must have fallen in the rubble.

He would have killed them both if Vera hadn't had her trusty backpack, but she couldn't leave him to die—no matter what he truly deserved.

Besides, his testimony would be needed to clear Verity's name—and to save Vera from the hangman.

"Oh, hell," Jericho muttered as if he'd read her thoughts. Between them, they reached down and grabbed the large man by his waistband, raising him to his feet.

He sagged against Vera, almost driving her to her knees.

Jericho's generosity was used up. "Stand up and walk, you lousy bastard, or I'll kick your butt all the way down the mountainside."

The big man must have believed him, because he obeyed Vera's order to hang on to her knapsack. Once more the unlikely threesome staggered forward.

Hobbling under the strain of their combined weight, she led the race to the entrance, praying aloud that there was still time. Praying there wasn't another obstacle lying unseen in their path.

They were only ten feet from the opening when an enormous explosion rocked through the narrow passage.

The timbers overhead creaked and shivered. Small embedded rocks worked free from the hard-packed walls and ceiling and rained down on their shoulders and heads.

Vera threw her hands up to shelter herself as a deluge of rubble and choking dust almost drowned them.

Greavy's hand slipped from her shoulder and he started to sag to the earth. She knew they had only seconds before the entire structure, now so badly weakened by the blast, came down upon their heads.

The corrupt physician was about to die in his own trap.

Jericho, who couldn't see the doctor had fallen, tugged at her arm and she knew she should just abandon Greavy to his fate. But despite all the pain and suffering he'd caused, the deaths and destruction, she still couldn't leave a living creature to suffocate.

Summoning the last vestiges of her strength, she clutched Greavy's arm and dragged him along behind as they raced the final few feet to the mine opening.

They barely cleared the timber-framed mouth of the mine when the entire structure shuddered one last time and collapsed in a seething volcano of dust and rocks.

For the longest time they lay where they fell, lacking even the fragment of energy needed to crawl to safety. It was over.

THREE DAYS LATER, Jericho came into the sitting room where Vera was enjoying her morning coffee.

"They just put Greavy on the train."

"He's healed enough to stand trial?"

Jericho shrugged. "He doesn't think so. But miners come home every day with more scrapes and bruises than he had. I'm afraid he didn't get much sympathy."

She twirled her spoon in her cup. "What do you think will happen to him? I mean, do you think he'll go the gallows?"

"Nah." Jericho snorted in disgust. "A fine upstanding citizen like Doc Greavy? Remember, there's not a shred of real evidence against him."

Vera's expression made her eyebrows dip in a frown. "Then why did he confess so readily?"

Jericho clenched his fist and blew on his knuckles. "A little friendly persuasion."

At Vera's dismay, he laughed and quickly recanted.

"Don't worry, I didn't touch him. Didn't have to. First of all, everyone in town knew he was out that night—delivering Mrs. Nesbitt's baby. A bad storm was brewing, no one else was out on that mountain."

"But that's only circumstantial," she argued.

"True. But a lot of little circumstances add up to a pretty complete picture. Greavy must have stopped by the cabin on his way from Nesbitt's, and gotten into an argument with Rafe. I imagine Rafe would have been pretty ornery waking up with a throbbing head and discovering his whole family had taken off."

"I imagine."

"Anyway, I figure they got into an argument, Doc shot him and then decided to take advantage of everyone's mistaken belief that Verity had killed him. Since the whole family had taken off to the res, he figured there wouldn't be a soul left to dispute that she'd shot him."

"Then when *I* showed up..."

"Exactly. Greavy couldn't let you have your day in court because he was too afraid Min-e-wah and the boys would come back to testify on your behalf. Anyway, when I told him we had the evidence of his partnership with Rafe, and that we would bring the entire family back from the reservation, he kind of folded. Admitted he and Rafe got into a helluva fight over controlling interest in the mind. Course, Doc's story is that he shot Rafe in self-defense."

"In the back?" Vera asked incredulously.

"Who's to argue? Rafe's long buried, all the witnesses are gone and Greavy himself certified the man's death. He'll tell his story, present a couple witnesses as to Rafe's lousy temper and probably draw a mild sentence for manslaughter.''

"That's not fair! He was willing to let Verity—me—hang for murder.''

Jericho patted her shoulder. "I wouldn't worry too much. Don't forget, he assaulted me and tried to blow both of us up in the Balbriggan. Plus he has Sheriff Hamblin to account for. Add our testimony to all the other circumstantial evidence and I've no doubt the judge is going to give him a long rest at the state's expense.''

Vera set her cup on the saucer and tugged Jericho's hand until he sat across from her. "What about Verity? What's happened to her?''

He shook his head slowly. "I don't know. I gave her money the other night but…but somehow I had the impression she wasn't planning on going to the reservation. She always had a yen to live in the city.'' He shrugged. "Maybe she's on her way to San Francisco.''

Closing her eyes, Vera recalled the references in Verity's journal to the "silver shoe.'' Had the girl traveled through time to the twentieth century and found it to her liking? Maybe, Vera thought with a smile, Verity had found her way to the future before the silver horseshoe was destroyed in the explosion and was living in Vera's apartment. Maybe right this moment the girl was snuggling a cat named Squiggles.

"We'll probably never know for sure what became of her,'' Jericho said, as if reading her thoughts.

"A true mystery." Vera smiled. "The stuff legends are built on. Might be good for tourism someday."

"Tourists? In Jerome?" Jericho chortled and slapped his knee. "That's a good one. Maybe we ought to change your act. 'Vera LaFleur, the comic chanteuse.'"

She threw her crumpled linen napkin at him. "You forget—I know the future. You can't argue with me."

He leaned back and surveyed her with his unflinching gaze. "Oh, sugar, you don't know the whole future. Trust me, I've got a few surprises in store for you."

Trailing her finger around her empty cup, Vera avoided his steady gaze. "So what happens now?"

"What do you mean?"

Looking up now, she swiped a film of moisture from her eyes. "What happens to me? I can't go back home, and I can't live here as Verity McBride, I'd feel like a fraud."

"You don't have to pretend to be Verity. With Doc's backing I convinced the boys that it was all a case of mistaken identity. Told 'em you were Verity's cousin from Frisco, Vera LaFleur. Course I imagine we could change that last name. If you've a mind to, that is."

Vera reached across the table and lightly caressed his hand. "I owe you so much. And I'm sorry to complain. It's just that…that losing my entire identity, losing my past, makes me feel…like an orphan. I've never felt more completely alone."

Jericho rose and moved behind her, his warm fingers gently massaging the knotted muscles at her neck. He bent down and touched his lips to the tender spot at her nape. "You're not alone. Not unless you want to be. I wouldn't blame you, though, if you wanted to get as far from me as you could. I should have believed you. I knew you weren't crazy, I just didn't understand."

She turned around and rubbed her cheek across his hand. "It doesn't matter."

"Yes, it does. Far-fetched as your story sounded, I shouldn't have just dismissed it as a woman's fancies. That was wrong and I apologize."

Vera smiled to herself. Maybe there was hope for this chauvinistic cowpoke after all. "It happened to me and I still don't quite believe it."

Taking her hand he led her into the bedroom. She sat on the edge of the bed while he drew the curtains.

When the room was dim and cozy, he approached the bed. "What will your folks think when you never come back?"

She sighed. "My landlord will sell all my stuff, my friend Sheila will adopt my cat Squiggles. My sergeant, unfortunately, will waste untold hours trying to find me. But the only family I have, my mother...mom will never know I'm gone."

He dropped onto the bed and rested his head in her lap. "I know you made a deliberate choice when you wasted all that time untying me. And while I'm so grateful to you and for you, I'm really sorry you had to give all that up."

Vera knew what he wanted to hear; that *she* wasn't sorry. The truth was, she didn't know yet *how* she felt. She'd sentenced herself to spend the rest of her life in the distant past.

She wouldn't have the luxuries and freedoms that she'd always taken for granted. Nor would she be able to utilize the job skills she'd worked so long to acquire.

On the other hand, she had skills and knowledge these people couldn't imagine. She knew enough of what the future held that she might be a benefit. History books said that Jerome would burn to the ground twice over the next few years. Perhaps Vera's knowledge of that danger would save lives. Her first order of business, in fact, was to organize that volunteer fire brigade Jericho had mentioned. She'd made a conscious choice and she'd make it again.

Vera dropped her hands to caress Jericho's beloved face. "Losing you wouldn't equal a thousand years of an empty future."

He reached up and pulled her down beside him, his dark gaze brushing her face like a velvet cloud. "You still have a future. With me."

Drawing her lips to his, they kissed. A sweet, satisfying kiss that made a pact. A kiss that promised eternity.

At that moment, Vera knew he was right. Their future would be one that lovers would still be talking about a hundred years from now.

They're brothers by blood, lawmen by choice, cowboys by nature.

THE COWBOY CODE

The McQuaid brothers learned justice and honor from their father, the meaning of family from their mother. The West was always in their souls, but now it's the past they have to reckon with. And three women hold the keys to their future.

Don't miss this exciting new series from three of your favorite Intrigue authors!

McQUAID'S JUSTICE
Carly Bishop
January 1999

A COWBOY'S HONOR
Laura Gordon
February 1999

LONE STAR LAWMAN
Joanna Wayne
March 1999

Available at your favorite retail outlet.

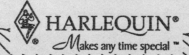

HARLEQUIN®
Makes any time special ™

If you enjoyed what you just read,
then we've got an offer you can't resist!

Take 2 bestselling love stories FREE!

Plus get a FREE surprise gift!

Amnesia...
an unknown danger...
a burning desire.
With

HARLEQUIN®

I N T R I G U E ®

you're just

A MEMORY AWAY

from passion, danger...
and love!

Look for all the books in this exciting new miniseries:

Missing: One temporary wife
#507 THE MAN SHE MARRIED
by Dani Sinclair in March 1999

Mission: Find a lost identity
#511 LOVER, STRANGER
by Amanda Stevens in April 1999

Seeking: An amnesiac's daughter
#515 A WOMAN OF MYSTERY
by Charlotte Douglas in May 1999

A MEMORY AWAY—where remembering the truth becomes a matter of life, death...and love!

Available wherever Harlequin books are sold.

COMING NEXT MONTH

#505 LONE STAR LAWMAN by Joanna Wayne
The Cowboy Code
Texas lawman Matt McQuaid had his hands full with Heather Lombardi.
Her search for her past incited trouble in his sleepy town, while the
woman herself excited the man behind the badge. He'd do anything to
wipe away her fears and keep her safe from a killer. But would he have
to blur the lines between honor and duty to protect the woman he loved?

#506 REDHAWK'S HEART by Aimée Thurlo
The Brothers of Rock Ridge
Forced to work together to catch a killer, lawman Ashe Redhawk
and beautiful FBI agent Casey Feist struck sparks off each other.
But when the sparks became a consuming fire of passion, Ashe was
compelled to choose between his heritage, and the woman who stirred
his soul.

#507 THE MAN SHE MARRIED by Dani Sinclair
A Memory Away...
She'd fallen down a mountain and barely survived. Eighteen months
later, Adam Ryser came to claim amnesiac Josy Hayes, saying he
was her husband and that he'd searched for her ever since she'd
mysteriously vanished. She'd be safe on his ranch, caring for his three
daughters—if only she could remember why she'd disappeared....

#508 A STRANGER'S WIFE by Paige Phillips
Jake Chastain was a woman's wildest dream—rich, handsome, sinfully
sexy. But someone was trying to kill him—while Meg Lindley pretended
to be his wife. Once Meg revealed her deception, could she ever win his
trust—and his heart?

Look us up on-line at: http://www.romance.net